### "Dance with me."

Nick moved closer and touched Allison's hair.

His voice sent shivers down her spine. She drew a long breath. "I—I don't dance."

"No? Come here."

Nick took her hand and drew her up against him.

They began to move in a slow, lazy circle. Allison tried to hold back, but it was impossible. He felt so hard and strong. She could feel his arms, his chest, his legs, all moving against hers, muddling her senses.

"I hope you've enjoyed the evening."

Allison felt cocooned in his embrace. "I haven't had an evening this nice in a long time," she said truthfully as he moved his hand over her back.

Neither had Nick. He couldn't ever remember feeling this way. It made him realize he didn't want the evening to end. In fact, he could see them like this forever. And that was a scary thought for a bachelor.

# STELLA BAGWELL

## The Best Christmas Ever

**HARLEQUIN**®
entertain, enrich, inspire™

ISBN-13: 978-0-373-36656-9

THE BEST CHRISTMAS EVER

Copyright © 1992 by Stella Bagwell

www.Harlequin.com

**Printed in U.S.A.**

**Stella Bagwell** has written more than seventy novels for Harlequin and Silhouette Books. She credits her loyal readers and hopes her stories have brightened their lives in some small way. A cowgirl through and through, she loves to watch old Westerns, and has recently learned how to rope a steer. Her days begin and end helping her husband care for a beloved herd of horses on their little ranch located on the south Texas coast. When she's not ropin' and ridin', you'll find her at her desk, creating her next tale of love.

The couple have a son, who is a high school math teacher and athletic coach. Stella loves to hear from readers and invites them to contact her at stellabagwell@gmail.com.

To the miracle of Christmas
and the gift of true love.

# Chapter 1

Nicholas Gallagher slowed his sports car as the blacktop gave way to dirt and the road took another sharp bend. To his right was the wide Arkansas River. Yet before he could catch a glimpse of the barges and towboats traveling the waterway, the road began to veer sharply away from the river and into wide, open fields. At the moment the land lay fallow. But Nick knew exactly how rich and fertile it would look come spring. He was on Gallagher land now—his family's farm.

Ahead of him, a county road grader was moving slowly, its slanted blade rolling the damp earth to one side of the road. Since the turn to the farm was only a half mile away, Nick downshifted and hung impatiently behind the vehicle.

Bright sunshine glinted off the red hood of his car, making it seem more like an early spring day instead of late December. Yesterday, when he'd left Fort Sill in western Oklahoma, the weather had been cold and wet. But the drive east had left the clouds and rain behind him.

It was a beautiful day, and he was almost home. *Home for Christmas.* It was a tradition for the Gallagher family to spend the holiday together. To eat, laugh, reminisce and generally make merry. Nick had always made it a point to return home and join in the celebration. But this year coming home for Christmas had taken on new meaning. His brother Sam was getting married and Nick was going to be the best man. He'd had a month to get used to the idea, but Nick still found it difficult to imagine his quiet, hardworking brother in love and about to get married.

While the grader continued to creep along in front of him, Nick looked things over. It was easy to see that Sam had been busy this past harvesting season. Even the land around the old Lee house showed signs of being worked. Nick remembered that particular section of land used to be farmed in watermelon and cantaloupe, but for the past few years it had lain dormant—mainly because Old Lady Lee had been in ill health and his father hadn't wanted to disturb her with the loud sound of tractors and the boiling dust plowing created.

Maybe the old woman had passed away, Nick thought. Although he couldn't remember his mother mentioning it in her letters.

Nick studied the square, wood-framed house sitting a hundred feet or so south of the road. The old Lee place was still unpainted and the tin roof was just as rusty as it had been when he'd come home last Easter. Still, it looked as though someone lived there. Curtains hung in the windows and wood was stacked neatly on the east end of the front porch.

However, Old Lady Lee swiftly left his mind as the cattle guard leading to the Gallagher farmhouse appeared on the right. With the road grader finally out of his path, Nick crossed the slatted entrance, then stepped hard on the accelerator. The sports car shot forward like a little red arrow. Dust roiled behind him and Nick chuckled as he pictured his mother's expression when she spotted him coming down the road. She'd scold him for driving recklessly, then scold him again for not letting the family know that he was coming home today.

At the back of the house, Nick jammed on the brakes, making gravel spray from the tires as the car skidded to a stop just short of the yard fence.

Inside the kitchen Ella glanced out the window, then darted an incredulous look at Kathleen. "My God, it's Nick! I'm going to thrash him! Did you see that? I'll bet that car isn't more than five inches from the fence!"

Before Kathleen could utter a word in defense of her brother, Ella dashed out the door to greet her son.

"Nicholas Gallagher! If I had your daddy's razor strop with me right now, I'd use it on you," she shouted as she ran down the steps.

Nick threw back his head and roared with laughter as he held his arms out to his mother. She ran straight into them and clutched her youngest child to her breast.

"Hello, Mom. Glad to see me?" he asked, bending his head to kiss her cheek.

Ella thrust him from her, then wagged her finger in his grinning face. "I'm glad to see you in one piece. Is that the way you drove coming home? Lord help us, it's a wonder you're alive! And what are you doing home today? It's two days before Christmas Eve!"

Laughing again, Nick threw his arm around his mother's shoulder and held her close. "Well, if I'm too early I can always leave and come back later."

"Not on your life!" Ella cried. "Sam's probably going to chain you to the bedpost as it is! He's tried to get through to you on the telephone all week."

"So," Nick said with a wicked grin, "I've had my brother a little worried that I wouldn't show up for the big event?"

"Nicholas!" Ella scolded. "Be serious! You know

how much your brother is looking forward to you standing up with him."

The door on the porch slammed, and Nick turned his head in time to see Kathleen scurrying down the steps toward him.

"Nick!" she squealed happily.

With his free arm, he reached out and pulled his sister against him. "Hi, sis! Don't tell me you knew I was coming?"

"Of course I didn't know! None of us did. Why didn't you call and tell us?" she asked, pinching his lean waist. "Sam's been out of his mind thinking you'd been shipped off to parts unknown."

"We've been out in the field for over a week on training maneuvers," Nick explained. "I couldn't get to a phone."

"And there's not one phone between here and Lawton? You could have at least called and warned us you were coming," Kathleen told him.

Nick's look told Kathleen just what he thought of her suggestion. "Are you crazy? And ruin my surprise?"

With a good-natured groan she said, "You haven't changed a bit."

"Would you really want me to, sis?" he asked, giving her an impish grin.

Kathleen moaned and rolled her eyes. "Mom, how are we ever going to put up with him and get ready for a wedding at the same time?"

"Well, we won't do it standing around here. Let's go in," Ella said, urging her son and daughter up the steps and into the house.

Inside the kitchen, Kathleen stood back with her hands on her hips and gave her brother a thorough looking over. "I guess you'll do," she said, her eyes full of love and laughter.

Ella wasn't nearly as kind. She poked a finger into his midsection. "You look thin. What has the army been feeding you—K rations three times a day?"

Laughing, Nick shook his head. "Mom, you're looking at a man in prime physical condition."

"If you say so, Sergeant Gallagher," Kathleen said teasingly. "How many push-ups can you do?"

"I won't tell. Sam might kill himself trying to outdo me." He glanced from his sister to look around the room. "Speaking of Brother Samuel, where is he? And where's my future sister-in-law? I'm dying to see if she's still as pretty as she used to be."

Ella waved her hand dismissively. "Actually, Olivia has been running her legs off getting ready for the wedding. But this afternoon she and Sam took time out to round up food and toys for the mission where she's been doing a little volunteer work."

Nick's brows arched in wonder. "Sam is out gathering food and toys? Instead of farming? Olivia must have really transformed the boy."

Ella gave her son an impatient look. "Your brother *can* do other things, you know. Besides, you might as well hear it right now. Olivia had a hard time of it over in Africa. Sam's trying to help her ease back into relief work. So don't be pestering her with a lot of questions about Ethiopia. You hear me?"

Nick stared at his mother. "You mean we have to handle her with kid gloves?"

"No, Nicholas. She isn't that fragile. I'm just telling you to be kind and…sensitive."

A beguiling grin suddenly spread across his face. "Now, Mother, you know that I know all about dealing with—"

"Yes. We know. Dealing with women," she interrupted, shaking her head.

Laughing, Kathleen crooked her arm through Nick's and tugged him over to the kitchen table. "Just wait until you see them together, Nick. I never thought I'd ever see Sam so happy. And Olivia is positively glowing."

Nick eased his six-foot frame into one of the wooden chairs at the table, then leaned back and crossed his legs at the ankles.

"So where's Dad?" he asked.

"He's down at the hog pen trying to build some sort of watering system that won't freeze. I guess he didn't hear you drive up," Kathleen said.

Nick told himself not to feel let down because his father wasn't around to greet him.

"He'll be in shortly," Ella told her son. "It's close to two o'clock and he can't go much longer than that without his afternoon coffee. He's going to be so surprised to see you."

"He must be getting soft in his older years," Nick said fondly. "I can remember when he'd have a fit if Sam and I quit for a soda."

Kathleen made a *tsking* noise with her tongue. "Don't you really mean a dip in the river that would end up lasting half of the afternoon?"

Nick made a face at his sister and she leaned over and mussed his dark auburn hair. "I'll bet you never tell those poor privates beneath you what a terror you used to be."

He grinned. "I'm not totally crazy, sis."

"Kathleen, come here and make coffee. You can talk to your brother from across the room. I've got to finish coloring this rice so it can be drying," Ella said as she wiped her hands on the edge of her apron. "Nick, do you want to bring in your bags now?"

"I have a whole trunkful of things out there. I'll get them later."

"You did bring your Class A's, didn't you? I know Sam will want you to wear them for the wedding," Kathleen said, referring to his dress military uniform.

Nick grinned, more to himself than at his sister. She was finally on the mend. Some of her old spark was back in her eyes and she was smiling and laughing again. It was wonderful to see.

"As a matter of fact, my Class A's were one of

the very first things I packed, sis. Along with your Christmas present, of course."

Kathleen instantly forgot the coffee. She came up behind her brother and, looping her arms around his neck, pressed her cheek against his. "You are going to tell me what it is, aren't you?"

Nick chuckled wickedly. "Not even a hint."

"Nick—" Kathleen began to plead, only to have Ella interrupt them.

"Kathleen, the coffee," she reminded her. "I'm sure Nick could use a cup after his long drive." The older woman wearily brushed back a wisp of hair. "I never realized getting ready for a wedding would be such a job. And with Christmas, too, I don't know if we're going to make it."

"Of course we'll make it. Nick's here to help now," Kathleen said happily.

Nick merely looked at the two women and laughed. "Me, help? I don't know anything about weddings. I'd rather march five miles in sleet and snow than go to a wedding."

"Scared all that love and commitment stuff might rub off, eh?" Kathleen teased.

His sister was so close to the truth it made Nick shift uncomfortably in his chair. "There's not a man alive that can truly say he likes weddings," Nick said defensively.

"The groom does, Nick. Isn't there someone back in Lawton expecting a marriage proposal from you?

You could make it a double wedding with Sam, you know, and save Mom a lot of extra work."

Nick looked pointedly at his sister. "I'm doing just fine, sis. Thanks anyway."

"I was only hoping," Kathleen said with a laugh.

Tired of sitting from the long drive across Oklahoma, Nick got to his feet and joined his mother and sister at the work island in the middle of the kitchen.

"Is Old Lady Lee still living?" he asked thoughtfully. "I see Sam planted the fields around her house this year."

"I'm sad to say she's in a nursing home now," Ella told him. "The poor dear could no longer see to take care of herself. And Allison, well, she has all she can do as it is. Still, the little thing feels so guilty about her grandmother."

Nick turned to his sister in confusion. "Who is this Allison she's talking about? The only person I ever remember living in that house was Old Lady Lee."

"Nick!" his mother scolded. "Quit calling her that. You know her name is Martha. My word, she fed you licorice every day of your young life."

"Yeah, and I hate licorice. But I kept going to see her thinking she'd give me something different," Nick confessed.

"Oh, my, you were awful," Kathleen said with a groan.

Nick gave her a wicked smile. "Awful good, sis,"

he teased, then asked, "So, who's living in Old Lady Lee's house now? There was wood on the porch."

His mother gave him an impatient look. "Why, Allison, of course! Martha's granddaughter."

"She'll be here tonight for supper," Kathleen explained, then with an impish smile, she reached up and grabbed his chin. "She's coming over to help us with some of the wedding preparations." Still holding on to his face, she glanced at Ella. "Look at him, Mother. Isn't he the most handsome thing? Who do you think is more handsome, him or Sam?"

Nick made a face at his sister and playfully swatted her hand away.

Ella's eyes were suddenly misty as she raised on tiptoe to kiss her son's cheek. "It's so good to have you home, Nick. Christmas wouldn't be right if you weren't here."

"Of course it wouldn't," Nick said with a waggle of his eyebrows. "If I weren't here, Santa would skip right over the Gallagher house."

Kathleen quickly switched on the coffeemaker and grabbed him by the arm. "Come on while the coffee perks, Nick, and look at the Christmas tree. We trimmed it just last night and it's absolutely beautiful."

Allison Lee clutched her three-year-old son's arm with one hand and waved at the day-care worker with the other. "See you in the morning, Cybil."

"You drive safely, Allison," the woman replied. "The radio reported rain moving in and the streets are so busy now—everyone is out Christmas shopping."

Everyone but her, Allison thought wearily as she hustled Benjamin to the car. She appreciated her job as a bank teller, but even when the holidays weren't going on, her paycheck did well to take care of the necessities of living.

Once Benjamin was safely buckled into his car seat, Allison started the car and headed home. Her route took her down busy Rogers Avenue. As she passed the huge shopping mall to her left, she noticed the parking lot was completely filled with cars.

With a wistful look in her green eyes, Allison thought of the few friends she would like to buy gifts for this Christmas. But it looked as though she'd been lucky to manage getting Benjamin's toys out of lay-away.

*Don't be feeling sorry for yourself, Allison. You have a warm roof over your head and a beautiful, healthy son. That's more than lots of people will have this Christmas.*

The reminder made Allison shake back her long strawberry blond hair with a proud toss of her head. She wasn't a person who whined or thought she deserved more than her fair share of things. She was doing the best she could as a single mother, and if her friends didn't understand, then they weren't her friends.

"I'm hungry, Mommy. Let's eat."

Allison glanced back at her son. He wasn't a chatterbox, but when he did talk, his meaning was clear.

"As soon as we get home I'll fix something, honey," she promised, then suddenly remembered she was supposed to go to the Gallaghers' tonight. Two days ago Ella had asked Allison if she could come over and help get things ready for Sam and Olivia's wedding. Then this afternoon she'd called again to tell her that Nick had surprised everyone by coming home early, and that they'd be expecting her and Ben by six-thirty.

Allison stifled a tired groan at the idea. She'd had an extremely long shift working the drive-in window at the bank, and the steady stream of customers had scarcely let up throughout the day. Her head was fuzzy and her neck and shoulders ached from sitting in one position. A can of soup and bed was all she needed or wanted tonight.

But the Gallaghers were so wonderful to her that Allison could hardly ignore the invitation. Since she'd moved into her grandmother's house, they'd taken her in and treated her almost like a family member. Benjamin felt at home there, too, and ever since S.T. had taken him for a ride on the tractor, he thought the older man was Santa Claus himself.

She glanced once again at her son. "How would you like to eat with Ella and S.T. tonight, Ben?"

"Yeah! Yeah! Tractor ride!"

Allison shook her head. "We can't ride the tractor tonight. It's too dark and cold. But I'll bet Jake and Leo will be somewhere around the house, and you know how much they like to play with you."

At the mention of the collies, Benjamin forgot about the tractor and began to talk about his last visit with Jake and Leo. Allison did her best to watch the heavy traffic and converse with her son at the same time. All the while she wondered what Ella and S.T.'s other son was like.

She'd heard different members of the Gallagher family mention him from time to time. She knew he was around twenty-four years old and had been serving in the military for the past six years. Ella had told her he was tall and handsome, but didn't every mother think her son was handsome? she asked herself, her eyes automatically filling with pride as she looked at Benjamin.

Thankfully, her son looked like her and not like the father who'd abandoned them long before Benjamin had been born. Larry didn't deserve to have a child resemble him. The only thing he deserved was to be treated in the same unpardonable way he'd treated her.

A few minutes later, she and Benjamin arrived at the old farmhouse. She quickly gave him a graham cracker to snack on while she rummaged through her closet for something to wear.

Most of her clothes were left over from her college days. All of them were well-worn, so there was no danger in her overdressing, she thought drearily.

Allison had gotten one year of higher education behind her before she'd met Benjamin's father, Larry. For a short time she'd allowed herself to be drawn in by his slick charms, his vows of love and the plans he had for their future. *Their future.*

She gave a deprecating snort at the idea. The only plan Larry had really had was to get her into his bed.

Up until a few months ago Allison had lived in Monroe, Louisiana. She'd been born there and had grown up there, but the place held nothing for her now. Her mother had died a long time ago. After his wife's death Clifford Lee had never cared much what happened to his daughter. Now that Allison had Benjamin, Clifford Lee had completely turned his back on her and his grandson.

She'd learned a hard lesson about men and responsibilities when Larry had walked out on her. But she'd learned an even harder one, she supposed, when her father had discarded her like an old rug he'd grown tired of stepping on. She could still remember him calling her a worthless embarrassment and that he wanted her out of his house and out of his life. He wasn't about to let her stick him with raising another kid.

Allison had been three months pregnant at the time and nearing the end of her sophomore spring semester at Northeast Louisiana University. She'd had no alternative but to move out of the house and drop the last of her classes. Up until Benjamin had been born, she'd worked as a bookkeeper for a lumber company. But after that she'd found it nearly impossible to pay her rent and have enough left from her paycheck to care for her son and herself. If it hadn't been for her Grandmother Lee, Allison didn't know where she would have been living now, or how she would have been surviving. The older woman had convinced her to come to Arkansas and live in her house. The place was old and a bit run-down, but at least it would take away the added burden of paying rent.

The past three years had been difficult ones for Allison, but since she'd moved to Arkansas in May things were slowly improving. She had a better job, a house to live in, and for the first time since her mother had died, she had a real family—her son and her grandmother.

The three of them would more than likely be the only family she would ever have. But that was just the way Allison wanted it. In her dictionary, the definition of man was trouble. And she didn't want trouble entering her life or her family's ever again.

"Oh my, that's really going to look pretty, girls," Ella said appreciatively, eyeing the long dining table. "Especially when we get the wedding cake and serving dishes on it."

Kathleen had covered the dark aged wood with a white lace tablecloth and Olivia had put together two flower arrangements of white and red poinsettias to flank the cake. Now the three women were standing back, admiring the effect of their handiwork.

"I think we need candles," Olivia said, just as Sam and Nick walked into the room.

The two brothers exchanged grins. "Does this woman of yours have eating or romancing on her mind?" Nick teased.

With a wicked smile on his face, Sam went to Olivia and slipped an arm around her waist. "Both, I hope," he said.

Kathleen continued to study the table with a critical eye. "You're right, Olivia. Candles would make it perfect."

"There's some in the kitchen pantry," Ella said. "And I think I can find a pair of silver holders in the buffet. They're probably tarnished, but we can clean them tonight with the rest of the silverware."

Earlier that afternoon, Nick had changed out of his military khaki. Now he looped his thumbs into the pockets of his blue jeans and rocked back on the heels of his cowboy boots as he eyed the elaborate table. "I thought this was just going to be a simple wedding. Am I really worth all of this?"

Sam groaned, and Kathleen said, "We didn't even know if *you* were actually going to be here or not."

Nick looked offended. "Sam knew I'd be here

even if the rest of you didn't think so. Isn't that right, Sam?"

Sam snorted. "I knew if you didn't show up, you'd better have a hell of an excuse."

Nick laughed at his brother's stern warning. Sam had always been the serious one. Even back when they'd been teenagers, it had been a major effort just to make him laugh. There'd been a time when Nick had wished his older brother would lighten up. But now that they'd grown older, Nick knew he wouldn't want his brother Sam any other way.

"Sam! Do you always talk to your brother like this?" Olivia asked, amazed.

Nick laughed. So did Ella as she came back into the room carrying two white candles. "Olivia, from the time Nick was old enough to walk, Sam has ordered him around and threatened him to within an inch of his life when he wouldn't obey. Nick's used to it."

"Never did mind you very much either, did I, big brother?" he asked with a playful poke at Sam's rib cage.

Sam gave him a dour look, but then his lips twitched with something close to a grin. "You want Allison to see you with a bloody nose?"

Nick cocked a brow at him, then touched the bridge of his nose. "I'd hate for you to have to get married with two black eyes. Olivia might want to postpone the honeymoon."

Sam laughed, then pressed a kiss against the curve of Olivia's cheek. "A couple of black eyes couldn't keep us apart, could they, honey?"

"Nothing could ever keep us apart," Olivia murmured.

Nick watched Olivia look adoringly at his brother and wondered what it would feel like to be loved like that. He'd never seen such love on anyone's face before and he felt a stab of jealousy in spite of himself.

"By the way, Mom," Kathleen said, glancing at her wristwatch, "is there anything I need to do in the kitchen before Allison arrives?"

"No. The sandwiches and snacks are all ready."

"What about a high chair for Ben?" Olivia asked.

Ella shook her head. "Ben thinks he's too big for a high chair. I usually let him sit on my granite roasting pan."

Nick was thoroughly confused as he tried to follow the women's conversation. "Allison has a small child?" he asked. "I thought she was an elderly woman. Why, Old Lady Lee is probably close to a hundred, isn't she?"

"Nicholas, I'm going to whack you if I hear you say 'Old Lady Lee' one more time. What will Allison think of you? Especially when I've told her that you're my most mannerly child."

"That's not saying too much for us, is it, Kathleen?" Sam commented.

Nick shook his head helplessly. To be honest, he

wished his mother hadn't invited anyone to the house tonight. He'd wanted to spend his first evening back home with just his family. Now he was going to have to make a point of being polite to some woman he'd never seen in his life. He liked meeting people but not tonight.

He almost wished he'd volunteered for Captain Logan's maneuvers drill and come home a day later. Toting an M16 over miles of wet, dark terrain seemed like a party compared to the evening ahead of him.

# Chapter 2

"Now listen, Ben, you must remember to be polite tonight," Allison told her son as she stepped up on the Gallaghers' back porch. "Ella thinks you're a good little boy."

"I am," he replied solemnly.

Allison didn't know whether to laugh or cross her fingers. "I know. That's why I'm counting on you to be on your best behavior."

"Where's Jake and Leo?" the child asked, tugging on his mother's arm just as she raised it to knock on the screen door.

"I don't know. We'll find out when we get inside,"

she told him, then reached to slick down the unruly cowlick at his forehead.

Kathleen answered the door and quickly ushered them into the house.

"Take off your coat, Allison, and I'll help Ben with his," Kathleen said, already kneeling to assist the small boy.

"My goodness, what a pretty dress. You didn't have to go to such pains for us," Ella spoke from across the room.

Allison's fair complexion became tinged with a delicate pink as she unconsciously smoothed a hand down the moss green skirt. "Thank you, Ella, but this dress has been in the washing machine more times than I could count."

"Come on to the den," Kathleen urged her. "I'm dying for you to meet Nick."

When Allison and Kathleen entered the den, Nick was standing with his back to the fireplace, listening quietly as his father and brother talked farming.

"Well, there's my little Ben," S.T. boomed out as he spotted the small boy. "Come here, son."

The redheaded child ran eagerly to the older Gallagher and climbed up on his lap, while Kathleen urged Allison farther into the room.

Nick tried not to stare, but he felt as if someone had whopped him over the head. The woman with his sister was nothing like he'd been expecting. She was young and lovely. Extremely lovely.

"Allison, this is my brother, Sergeant First Class Nicholas Gallagher. The infamous one, we all like to say," Kathleen added jokingly.

Allison moved forward and offered her hand to Nick. "It's nice to finally meet you," she said.

So this was Old Lady Lee's granddaughter! She had the most gorgeous red hair he'd ever seen. Or was it blond? Whatever color, the shoulder-length curly tresses went perfectly with her ivory white skin and sea green eyes. Why hadn't anyone told him a vision was living next to the Gallagher farm?

"Hello, Allison. And before we go any further, whatever my family has told you about me is definitely not true."

There was a sparkle in his dark blue eyes that Allison couldn't quite ignore. She found herself smiling back at him in spite of the warning signals going off in her head. "Actually, I didn't believe the part about you eating bullets for breakfast."

Nick's smile grew broader. "You were right. I wouldn't eat bullets unless I had cinnamon toast to go with them."

Across the room, Sam made a noise somewhere between a snort and a laugh. Deliberately ignoring his brother, Nick continued to hold Allison Lee's small hand in his. "Mom tells me you're Martha's granddaughter," he went on, careful to use the old woman's given name.

Allison looked back at Nick Gallagher. Ella had

been right when she'd described her son. He was a tall, handsome man. On first glance his closely cropped hair appeared almost black, but on second look she saw that it was actually a deep shade of auburn. Yet he didn't have the fair complexion of a redhead. In fact, his complexion was darker than Sam's or his father's. A result of his job, she supposed.

At the moment his lean, angular face was creased in a smile that dimpled his right cheek and displayed his straight white teeth.

Allison took a deep breath and pulled her hand from his. "That's right," she answered. "My father was Martha's only child."

"Nick," Kathleen spoke up, "why don't you get Allison a glass of wine, and I'll go see if Mom and Olivia need any help in the kitchen?"

"Sure thing," he said and crossed the room to pour the drink. When he turned around, he saw that Allison had taken a seat on the couch a couple of cushions from his brother.

"I wanted to thank you for the wood you left yesterday," she said to Sam. "You can't imagine how much it will help in heating the house. But I would like to pay you for it."

Sam shook his head at her just as Nick arrived with her drink. "I don't want your money, Allison. Consider the wood a Christmas gift from me," he said.

Nick offered Allison the wineglass. She accepted

it with a brief thank-you and a faint smile, then turned her attention back to Sam. Nick was amazed at the envy that knifed through him. She was looking at his brother as if he were dear and familiar. Maybe he was, Nick thought crossly. But Sam already had one beautiful blonde madly in love with him. Did he really need two?

"You're too generous, Sam."

Yes, far too generous, Nick thought dryly. He'd always wondered why women were drawn to Sam. His older brother had always been quiet and brooding, even cynical at times. Maybe they found him a challenge.

Hell, Nick thought, his good humor suddenly returning. He was a challenge himself. No woman had caught him yet. And no woman was ever likely to catch him. He was young and still having too much fun to be tied down by just one woman. Even one as lovely as Allison Lee.

"So how long have you been living in the old farmhouse?" Nick asked Allison as he took a seat on the arm of the couch.

"I moved in last May," she answered, trying not to notice how close he was to her.

He was nothing like Sam, she thought. Sam had always treated her like a friend. But this military man was sending her all sorts of dangerous signals. There was a reckless glint in his eyes that left her feeling decidedly edgy and wishing the night was over before it had even began.

"Allison is originally from Louisiana," Sam explained.

Nick wondered why Allison Lee had left Louisiana and moved into her grandmother's old house. And where was her husband?

Curiously, he glanced at her left hand to check for a ring. There was none. She wasn't wearing any jewelry that he could see, yet she appeared anything but plain. She was like a jewel herself—full of vibrant color and a touch of mystery.

Olivia came into the room and took a seat on the arm of the couch beside Sam. Allison smiled warmly at the woman who'd become her friend over the past month.

"Are you nearly ready for the wedding?" Allison asked her.

Olivia laughed softly. "Right now I think we have things in an organized sort of chaos."

"Well, I'll be glad to help anyway I can," Allison assured her.

Olivia exchanged glances with Sam, then looked back at Allison. "Actually, there was something I wanted to ask you," Olivia began carefully.

Allison looked at her expectantly. "Yes?"

"Sam and I talked it over and we'd love for you to be my bridesmaid."

Allison couldn't have been more shocked. "Oh, but surely Kathleen is—"

"Going to be my maid of honor. So please say you will. I know it's a little late to ask but it would please Sam and me if you would agree."

Allison was overwhelmed. These people wanted to include her in something that was obviously a family affair. She couldn't quite believe it. "Oh, Olivia, I—"

Embarrassed, especially because she knew Nick was listening, she broke off. But then she realized there was nothing she could say except the truth. "I'm so touched that you want me to be your bridesmaid, but to be honest I—don't have a dress that would be—"

"Don't worry about a dress," Olivia quickly assured her. "What you wear isn't important. Is it, darling?" she asked, glancing down at Sam.

He shook his head. "Olivia isn't worried about a person's clothes."

Sensing how awkward she must be feeling, Nick felt compelled to lighten the mood. "That's right, Allison, or she definitely wouldn't be marrying Sam," he told her. "He's a true farmer. He wears long johns until April. I just hope the neck doesn't show when he puts on his tie."

"Sure, Nick," Sam said while the rest of them laughed.

"I won't take no for an answer," Olivia said when

the laughter died away. "Besides, Kathleen has all sorts of dresses you can wear if need be."

Allison smiled and lifted her hands in a gesture of compliance. "Then I'd be honored to be your bridesmaid."

"That's wonderful!" Olivia exclaimed.

From across the room, S.T. broke into the conversation. "Sam, Benjamin wants to know where Jake and Leo are."

Sam motioned for the boy to come to him. Benjamin approached the couch shyly, one finger stuck in the side of his mouth. Nick could see his resemblance to Allison and for the second time he wondered about the child's father.

"The dogs are down at the barn, Ben. They're asleep on the hay."

"Why?"

"Because it's cold and dark and they're sleepy," Sam explained.

"I'm not sleepy," Benjamin said, in a way that implied the dogs shouldn't be sleepy, either.

Amused, Sam got to his feet and held his hand out to the boy. "I know where there's another dog. Come on, I'll find him for you. Want to come with us, Olivia?"

Ben placed his hand in Sam's and the three of them left the room. Nick quickly slid off the arm of the couch and took up his brother's vacated seat.

Allison took a sip of her wine and crossed her

legs. She wished Ella would call them in to supper. She felt like a bird cornered by a persistent tomcat.

"Benjamin is a fine looking boy. How old is he?"

"Three."

"He seems fond of Dad."

"S.T. entertains him."

Nick leaned back and crossed his ankles. He wanted to appear casual and uninterested, but found it impossible to keep his eyes off her. The green dress she was wearing was made of something soft and clingy. The neck was high, but the bodice was fitted, outlining her rounded breasts. She had a lush figure, full at the breasts and hips, narrow and trim at the waist. She was the kind of woman who could turn a man's mind to a pile of mush in a matter of minutes. In fact, his was getting pretty mushy, he realized with a start.

Allison could feel Nick's eyes making a slow appraisal of her. A part of her resented it, but a foolish part of her was flattered that he might find her attractive.

After a few moments of silence passed, Nick asked, "Do you always talk this much?"

She looked at him, her green eyes slightly veiled by thick brown lashes. "I'm afraid I'm not that much of a talker. Especially after a day like today."

His brows lifted with curiosity. "And what was your day like?"

She knew he was merely making friendly conversation, so why did she feel so cornered by each question he put to her? "It was very busy. I work as a bank teller, you see, and today was my turn at one of the drive-in windows."

"Hmm. I suppose at this time of year it's even worse," he mused, then smiled. "Are you ready for Christmas? I'll bet you're one of those people who has her shopping done weeks ahead of time."

She glanced away from him as his words reminded her just how meager her shopping would be this Christmas. "No... I'm one of those last minute shoppers," she said, while twisting the stem of her glass between her fingers.

*Damn Nick, why did you have to mention shopping?* he asked himself. She'd already admitted she couldn't afford to buy herself a dress. No doubt she could afford little more than necessities.

"I was sorry to hear your grandmother is in a nursing home," he said, deciding to quickly change the subject. "I can't imagine her not living in the old farmhouse anymore. When I was a small boy I went to see her every day."

"I know. She speaks of you from time to time."

Nick was surprised. "Does she really? I would have thought she'd forgotten me by now."

A faint smile touched Allison's lips. "She said you were a pesky little thing, but when you grew up and stopped coming to see her, she missed you."

Nick wondered why he suddenly felt a pang of

guilt because he'd stopped visiting the old woman. "I'd like to see her while I'm here," he said suddenly. "Is she well enough to receive visitors?"

Allison was taken by complete surprise. She hadn't expected him to inquire about her elderly grandmother, much less want to see her. "Actually, she's a very healthy ninety-two, except for her sight, that is. And she loves visitors."

Allison's attention was caught by the sound of running feet. Before she could turn her head in their direction, Benjamin was racing around the couch toward her.

"See my dog, Mommy!" he exclaimed excitedly, then thrust the large stuffed toy at his mother.

Allison reached out and patted the floppy-eared version of a basset hound. It was limp and a little ragged in places, but was still holding together. Apparently the dog had been a childhood favorite of at least one of the Gallagher children. "He's very pretty. Did you thank Sam and Olivia for getting him for you?"

Benjamin nodded with great exaggeration and Nick grinned at the boy and the old familiar dog. "That's Buddy," Nick said, nodding his head toward the dog. "Kathleen dragged that dog from here to Texas. She wouldn't even go to the dentist without him."

"Who did I take to the dentist?" Kathleen asked

curiously as she walked up on the last of the conversation.

"Buddy," Sam explained. "I got him out of the closet so that Ben would have something to play with."

"Good," Kathleen said, reaching to playfully tousle Benjamin's hair. "He smells better than Jake and Leo. And he has better dog manners."

Puzzled, Benjamin looked around the group of adults. "What's that, Mommy?"

"Come here, son," S.T. said as chuckles floated around the room. "I'll tell you all about dog manners and little boy manners."

"You'll have to do that while we eat," Ella said from the doorway. "Everything is ready and waiting."

The announcement caused a stir as everyone got to their feet and moved to the kitchen. Allison led Benjamin by one hand, while he clutched the stuffed dog to him with the other. But once they reached the table she talked him into letting her put the dog under his chair.

Once Allison finally had her son settled safely on Ella's roasting pot, she looked up to see Nick holding a chair out for her.

"You don't mind sitting by me, do you, Allison?"

However could she answer that when the whole Gallagher clan seemed to be looking at her? "No—

of course not," she stammered, feeling a telltale heat warm her cheeks.

"I assure you, I'm like Buddy—I have good eating manners," he said with a wink.

"I wouldn't be so sure about that, Allison," Sam warned from the other end of the table. "He'll steal the food off your plate if you aren't watching."

Allison allowed Nick to seat her, while across the table, Ella said, "If I remember right, Sam, you always dropped most of your food under the table for Sally."

"That's right," Kathleen added. "No wonder the poor dog died. She was so overweight she could hardly walk."

Sam shook his head at his sister. "She could hardly walk because she had arthritis. And what about all the candy you gave her?"

"She loved chocolate candy—" Kathleen countered, only to have Ella tap her fork loudly against her plate.

"Oh, my word. Let's not start arguing about Sally now!"

Nick and Ella exchanged knowing glances while Allison sat quietly and watched. She'd never been around a big family before, but she'd often wondered what it would be like to have a brother or sister to talk and laugh with, parents that truly loved her.

Her mother had loved her, but her death had left Allison alone with a father who hadn't wanted her.

As a result she'd grown up starved for love and affection. It was no wonder that she'd fallen so easily for Larry's lies. She'd soaked up the physical love he'd given her and refused to see that it was only skin-deep.

"Your mother is right. It's time to eat instead of argue," S.T. said sternly, although the crooked grin on his face revealed just how much he was enjoying seeing all his family together.

"Eat! Eat!" Benjamin repeated.

"Ben! Shh!" Allison scolded lightly.

Nick chuckled. "I think Ben is smarter than the whole bunch of us."

"Say grace, Sam, and let's get some food on the boy's plate," S.T. instructed his older son.

The meal was full of boisterous conversation and laughter. Allison was content to merely eat and listen. And try not to notice the man beside her. She tried especially hard not to notice the way his eyes lingered on her face each time he passed her something. But try as she might she could not ignore the curiosity she had about him, or the strange rush of excitement it gave her to have him sitting beside her.

If Allison hadn't known beforehand that he was a military man, she probably wouldn't have guessed him as one. But as she studied him covertly, she could see little things about him that looked military. Like the neatness of his clothes, his proud, erect carriage, the trim hardness of his body.

He was very unlike Sam, she thought. And she wondered what had made him want to be in the army. Had he disliked farming, or was it that he loved being a soldier more?

Benjamin's small hand tugging at her arm brought Allison out of her musings. She saw that her son was finished eating and growing impatient to leave the table.

After excusing them both, she took Benjamin to the den and settled him and the stuffed dog on a braided rug not far from the fireplace. She'd just taken a seat on the couch to wait for the others when Nick walked in carrying three small plates.

"You haven't had dessert yet," he explained at her look of surprise.

"You shouldn't have bothered," Allison insisted. "I'm already stuffed."

"Mother's feelings would be hurt if you didn't eat a piece of cake. She thinks of it as one of her specialties."

Nick handed her the dessert plate holding the thick slice of cake, gave one to Ben and then took a seat next to her.

"Everything Ella cooks is a specialty," Allison said as she dipped a fork into the cake. "But you don't have to sit in here with me, Nick. I'm just a neighbor, not a guest that has to be entertained."

His sudden smile was crooked, as though he found her words amusing. "You don't have to make such a point of getting rid of me, either."

A blush spread across Allison's fair cheeks. Had it really been so obvious that she wanted to avoid his company? She hoped not. She didn't want him to think she disliked him. But then, she didn't want him to think she was interested in him, either. "I wasn't. I mean—I just meant that your family will be wanting you to finish eating with them."

Nick shifted around on the cushion so that his back was resting against the arm of the couch and his knee nearly touching Allison's thigh. She felt every nerve inside her coil to sudden attention.

"I'll be here until after Christmas. They'll all be sick of my company by then. Besides, I'm curious."

Without looking at him, she lifted the cake to her mouth. "Oh? About what?" she asked, although she could already guess. He'd probably been wondering throughout the evening about Benjamin, and why a young single woman like herself had a child.

"About my family," he answered. "Not one of them mentioned to me that a beautiful woman had moved next door. I wonder why that is?"

Allison's eyes remained on the fat slice of cake she was holding. "Probably because I'm not beautiful," she murmured, hoping he couldn't sense the rapid beat of her heart.

She knew she was behaving like a complete idiot, but she wasn't used to dealing with men or compliments. At least not since her ordeal with Larry. Since then, she'd steered clear of any kind of male attention.

Nick laughed softly and took a bite of his cake. He could see that he bothered her. He didn't exactly understand why, but the fact that he did pleased him enormously.

"You don't like me much, do you?"

His question was so unexpected that her head jerked up. "What?"

He gave her a patient smile. "I said that you—"

"No, I mean, why would you—why do you think that?"

He smiled again, knowingly this time. "Oh, it probably has something to do with that ice I see in your eyes every time you look at me."

Embarrassed, she jerked her eyes away and looked across the room to where Ben still sat playing on the rug. "You're misreading me," she said as casually as she could manage. "How could I not like you? I don't even know you."

"That's true," he said thoughtfully, then took another bite of cake. "At first I thought it was simply because I was a man. But you seem to like Dad, and it's obvious that you like Sam."

"Of course I like Sam. He's a dear man." Since she'd moved into her grandmother's old house, Sam had done things for her that she could never possibly have managed on her own. Like when he'd fixed the broken water line in the bathroom and patched the roof where it had leaked near the foot of her bed. She never forgot a kindness and Sam had been kind to her.

Nick snorted, but the sound was softened with a grin. "Believe me, Allison. Sam's not a dear. He's a bear."

Tilting her head to one side, she looked at him. "Really? Then what are you?"

His dark blue eyes were suddenly full of laughter. "Why, Miss Lee, I thought you knew I was a soldier."

He was playing with her, Allison thought. But, surprisingly, she didn't resent the fact. Why should she? she asked herself. Nick was more or less a stranger and he'd be gone from here in a matter of days. He couldn't hurt her in any way. She felt a bit safer at the thought.

Smiling now, Allison sliced off another bite of cake. "And what kind of soldiering do you do? Do you sit behind a desk or are you out in the field?"

"A little of both."

"Do you like it?"

Nick shrugged. "I guess I like it. I've done it for six years."

He hadn't really answered her question. But Allison wasn't going to point that out to him. The last thing she wanted was for Nick Gallagher to get the idea she was interested in him.

## Chapter 3

A few moments later S.T. and Sam came into the den. Allison quickly excused herself to join the women in the kitchen. Ella brought out the silver polish and they all went to work cleaning the silverware and table pieces that would be used for the wedding reception. When that job was finished they went to work making bags of rice, cutting tiny little squares of fine red netting, filling them with dry rice and tying the tops with satin ribbons. It was a painstaking job, but Ella said it wouldn't be a wedding unless the guests had rice to throw at the bride and groom.

None of them realized they'd been working for nearly two hours until Sam and Nick came into the room.

"Olivia," Sam said, placing a gentle hand on her shoulder. "You're going to be worn-out. Why don't you call it quits for tonight?"

Ella quickly agreed, saying they could all use another round of cake and coffee.

"I'd really better be going," Allison said quickly. "Ben needs to be in bed. Especially with tomorrow being a workday for me."

"Your son is sound asleep," Nick told her. "I think Dad told him one too many farming stories."

Allison glanced to where he was standing across the table from her and smiled briefly. "Thank you for keeping an eye on him. I'll just go start the car and let it be warming before I get him."

She was over by the door, pulling on her coat, when Nick walked up behind her. Allison knew it was him even before he spoke and her heart began to thud heavily against her breast.

"I'll go start your car," he said.

Her hands stilled on the button at her neck. His voice was so coarse and deep, so totally masculine that it sent shivers down her spine. "That's okay. I'm used to doing it."

"Nonsense. Give me the key."

Not wanting to appear ungrateful to the rest of the Gallaghers, Allison pulled her keys out of her coat and handed them to him.

He went out the door with a grin on his face while

Allison took a deep breath and headed to the den for her son.

She'd told everyone good-night and was carrying Ben across the breezeway when Nick suddenly appeared in front of her.

"The car is running," he said. "Let me carry him for you."

"Really, Nick, I can—"

Before she could say more, Nick reached for the sleeping child. Allison could do little more than hand him over. As she did, her fingers inadvertently touched Nick's arm. The warmth and strength she felt beneath the thin material of his shirt left a strange feeling in the pit of her stomach. She tried her best to ignore it as they made their way through the kitchen to the back door.

"Oh, Allison," Kathleen called, hurrying to catch her before she stepped onto the porch. "You forgot to take Buddy."

Allison hesitated, then shook her head as Nick's sister thrust the floppy-eared dog toward her. "No, I couldn't take your dog."

Kathleen laughed at Allison's protest. "Why ever not? Ben loves him."

"I know. But the dog is obviously your keepsake."

Kathleen smiled fondly at the dog in her hand. "I've had him forever. Now I want to give him to Ben."

Maybe it was just a worn-out toy, Allison thought.

But she knew how much she'd missed her own keep-sakes. "That's very sweet of you, Kathleen, but I'd feel awful about taking him. You might want to give him to a child of your own someday."

As soon as the words were out Allison knew she'd said something wrong. Pain, or something close to it, flickered in Kathleen's eyes and her hands gripped the furry dog. "That's something that won't be happening," she said in a husky voice, then thrust the dog into Allison's hands and hurriedly turned away. "Take good care of him. That's all I ask," she called as she left the room.

Allison looked up at Nick, who was standing just outside on the porch. His expression was solemn.

"What's wrong? What did I say?" Allison asked anxiously.

Nick shook his head. "It's not your fault. Come on. I'll tell you later."

Allison hurried across the backyard and to her car so that she could have the door already open for Nick. After he'd carefully placed the child on the back seat, he turned and opened the front door on the passenger side.

"I'll go with you to carry him in," he explained.

Allison's heart was suddenly flopping like a fish out of water. "It's all right. I'm used to carrying him," Allison assured him, then climbed behind the wheel.

Nick ignored her protest and joined her on the front seat anyway. Once he'd shut the door, he looked over at her bemused face. "Let's go, woman! It's freezing in here."

Frowning, Allison thrust the car into reverse, then headed down the road. Relax, she quickly told herself. It wasn't like he was going to make a pass or anything. He was just here to help her with Benjamin.

She glanced over at the man sitting only a few inches away from her. "I hope I didn't upset Kathleen too much over the toy. It was so generous of her that I..." Allison sighed, then started again. "I guess I reminded her of her dead husband when I mentioned her having children, didn't I?"

He shook his head. "No, it wasn't that. Kathleen and her husband were never able to have children."

Allison wished she could kick herself. "Oh, my, I'm so sorry. What must she think of me?"

"You didn't know. She understands that."

"I didn't know. But, oh, my," she said again, feeling an unbearable sadness for Nick's sister. "Please explain to her, will you?"

"I will. But you should forget it. I'm sure Kathleen already has."

By now they had reached the short driveway to her house. Allison pulled in slowly and parked on the west side beneath the bare branches of a huge sycamore tree.

She'd left the door to the house unlocked and a lamp on in the living room. With Ben in his arms,

Nick followed her through the small shadowy rooms to a bedroom at the back, then stood to one side as she pulled the covers on a half bed equipped with a safety rail.

After Nick had gently laid the boy on the smooth sheet, Allison removed his outer clothing, then pulled a heavy comforter up over his shoulders and placed a kiss on his cheek. It was a sight that called up Nick's own childhood, when his mother had done the same nightly ritual for him. He'd always felt utterly loved by his mother. Just as Ben probably did. For it was more than obvious that Allison was devoted to her son. It made him wonder if she was still devoted to the child's father. Wherever he was.

Turning from the bed, Allison almost bumped into him and nearly lost her footing trying to avoid a head-on crash into his broad chest. Nick caught her arm to steady her.

"S-sorry," she stammered a bit breathlessly. "I didn't realize you were still here."

The room was dark, but there was enough of a glow coming from the yard light outside for Allison to see his mouth curve into a crooked smile.

"I figured I'd better follow you back through the house so you could lock up," he said.

Allison was acutely aware of his fingers, the warmth that radiated from them. Although he was holding her gently, she somehow knew the grip of his hand could be powerful if he wanted it to be so.

She wasn't used to big strong men, and certainly not big, strong, good-looking men like Nick Gallagher. And that was the only reason she was having these strange reactions to him, she told herself.

"I'll—just give me a moment and I'll drive you back to your house," she told him.

She made a move toward the door. Nick was forced to release her arm and follow. Although he realized with a start that he would have been perfectly happy to keep standing there close to her in the darkness. Perfectly happy to simply hold her arm and look down at her face.

*That's not your style, Nick. You're a man of action, not a sentimental, romantic sop.*

"I couldn't ask you to leave Ben," he told her while trying to sort out the strange things wheeling around in his head.

"It only takes a minute. Two at the most. I'm outside at the clothesline longer than that."

The sweet, erotic scent of jasmine drifted to him as he followed her through the darkened hallway. Nick took a deep breath and tried to cleanse his wayward thoughts. "Still, I wouldn't hear of it. I'll jog back."

They were in the living room now. Allison stood stiffly with her hands folded in front of her. Actually, they weren't folded, they were clenched, but she hoped he wasn't able to see her nervousness in the low lamplight.

Nick took a moment to look around the long room. There was a faint glow of dying embers in the shallow fireplace, a few steps away from it a cherry-wood rocker. Nick stared at the old, familiar chair. "That was Martha's old rocker. I remember her having it out on the porch in the summertime."

The fact that he remembered both touched and surprised Allison. She'd been speaking the truth when she'd said her grandmother had often mentioned Nick. But there'd been times when she'd wondered if those accounts of his visits had been just the imagination of a lonely old woman. Now that she'd met Nick, she knew they hadn't been.

"You really did come to see her, didn't you?" she said, her voice touched with wonder.

He turned his head to look at her, then almost wished he hadn't. She was like a vision with the faint glow of light haloing her long, red hair and outlining the lush curves of her body. Nick had known lots of women. Some of them had even been beautiful. But none of them had affected him quite like this one. Nick couldn't understand it. Why did this one make him feel so giddy, like a schoolboy with sweaty palms?

"Of course I did. Dad used to get angry with me because I spent so much time over here instead of doing my chores."

A faint smile touched her face. "And why did you

spend time with Grandmother? To get out of doing your chores?"

Nick laughed softly. "It sounds that way. But actually, no. My grandparents lived in Texas and I rarely got to see them. I guess Martha was like having a grandmother here at home. She'd give me licorice, which I hated with a passion, but I'd eat it anyway just so she would tell me Civil War stories."

"Why didn't you tell her you hated licorice?"

Nick's expression was suddenly sheepish. "I didn't want to hurt her feelings."

Allison couldn't imagine this sergeant in the army being worried about such a thing. "What about Sam? Didn't he want to hear Civil War stories, too?"

Nick shook his head and jammed his hands in the front pockets of his jeans. "Sam was always content to work on the farm. Whether it was planting time or harvesting time, he wanted to be in on the doing of it."

"And you didn't?"

"Not always." Which was true enough, Nick thought. But he'd never been as good at it as Sam. Sam had been able to plow a straight row from the time he was twelve years old, whereas Nick had always ended up daydreaming and straying off course. S.T., hotter than the devil himself, would come out to the fields and order Nick off the tractor and Sam up in the driver's seat. It was a scenario that had been repeated over and over during their growing up years. Sam was still in the driver's seat as far as the farm was concerned, Nick realized. This year his brother had taken over sole responsibility of running the farm. Nick didn't know how he felt about that. Actually, he tried not to think about it at all.

"What are you doing here, Allison?"

"I beg your pardon?"

"Why are you living here in this old house, on land that has long since been sold to the Gallaghers?"

She unconsciously took a step toward him. "Does that bother you?"

His bark of laughter told her what he thought of her question. "Not hardly." But *she* bothered him. Bothered the hell out of him.

"Then why do you ask?" she wanted to know.

A deep smile dimpled his cheeks. Allison suddenly wondered how many women had seen that same smile and been charmed by it.

"Ask your grandmother. She'll tell you I was always a nosy little boy."

But he was no longer a little boy, Allison thought. Not by the furthest stretch of imagination. Deciding to be direct with him, she said, "I live here because I like being near my grandmother, and because it's all I can afford."

*All I can afford.* She hadn't said we, she'd said I, so that meant there was no him—no husband or live-in lover. Nick suddenly felt elated.

"Sorry if I seemed too nosy. Here, let me build up

your fire before I leave. It's going to be cold tonight. We might even have snow by morning."

"Uh—no," she quickly blurted as he headed toward the dying fire.

He looked over his shoulder at her, his expression quizzical. "What is it? What's wrong?"

Allison felt herself blushing, then told herself it was stupid to be embarrassed because she had to be frugal. "I can't afford to burn wood all night. And I don't intend to take advantage of Sam's generosity and ask him to cut more."

In spite of her words, Nick knelt on the hearth and began to stack a generous amount of small logs on the hot coals. "Sam likes to cut wood. It keeps his shoulders broad."

It was on the tip of her tongue to ask him what kept *his* shoulders broad, but she stopped herself just in time.

"Do you know you have a bad habit?"

He shook the logs with an iron poker before turning his head to look at her. "Just one? I must be improving in my old age. So what is this bad habit of mine?"

She unclenched her hands and planted them on her hips. "You ignore a person's, or more specifically, my wishes."

Flames began to lick around the logs. Nick straightened to his feet. "In the army we don't know anything about wishes, only orders."

Allison shifted her eyes to his face, then felt the sudden need to swallow. "Then perhaps I should order you."

"To do what?"

Why did the house suddenly seem so quiet, so small? "To—to not do the opposite of what I ask you to do."

She was becoming flustered and Nick was enjoying every minute of it. Even in the dim light he could see that her green eyes were sparkling, and the defiant set of her chin made her seem just that much more womanly. "I don't recall you *asking* me to do anything," he said with exaggerated innocence.

The urge to groan loud and long had Allison lifting her eyes to the ceiling. "I'm not asking you to do anything." She shook her head. "Forget what I said. It's obvious we don't communicate very well."

Nick could see himself communicating with her very well, but not in the verbal sense. At the moment everything he was thinking and feeling was purely physical. Rising to his full height, he looked down at her. "Oh, I think we could communicate," he drawled, "if we put our minds to it."

The strange glimmer in his eyes put Allison instantly on guard and had her retreating a step backward. Communicate how? she suddenly wondered. With body language? The same way Larry had wanted to communicate with her?

Allison walked purposefully to the door. "Thank you for helping me with Ben and with the fire."

"You didn't want a fire," he reminded her, knowing she was politely dismissing him, but still wanting to keep their banter going.

"I know. But you made me one anyway."

And now she was wanting him to leave, he thought. If it had been any other woman Nick would have found a way to stay with her. But something had already told him that Allison Lee was not any other woman.

"I wouldn't worry about the wood if I were you," he said as he joined her at the door. "Santa will probably bring you a load for Christmas."

Her hand paused on the doorknob as she looked up at him. "I can't imagine a hardened military man believing in Santa Claus," she said. "I suppose next you'll be telling me that he visits your barracks every year."

Nick tried his best to look affronted. "Of course he does. Doesn't he come to see you?"

"He comes to see Benjamin."

"But not you?" he asked in disbelief.

"I suppose I haven't been good," she said, wishing he would leave and put this whole ridiculous conversation behind them.

It was hard for Nick to imagine this woman being anything but good. Most of the women he knew would have been giving him signals to stay. As it was, Allison was doing all she could to get him out the door.

"There's still a few days until Christmas. Maybe you could change your ways and put yourself in good standing with old St. Nick."

"I'll keep that in mind, Sergeant."

He moved a step closer, while the grin on his face deepened. Allison's hand slipped from the doorknob as she moved to one side and out of his path.

"It's Nick to you, Allison. Only my underlings are forced to call me Sergeant."

"Well, Nick, I'll do my best to change my bad ways before Christmas," she promised. Anything to get him out of here, she thought desperately.

Nick reached to open the door and saw pure relief sweep over her face. Did she actually find his company that hard to tolerate, or was it just men in general?

"Will I see you tomorrow?"

Would he see her tomorrow? Was he serious? "I doubt it," she said quickly. "I'll be working tomorrow."

"But you won't be working tomorrow night."

Allison unconsciously edged farther away from his tall form. "No, but—"

"Good. I see you don't have your Christmas tree up yet. We'll go find one for you."

Her awkwardness momentarily forgotten, she stared at him incredulously. "I don't think—"

Before she could finish, he opened the door. Cold wind blasted her in the face.

"Be ready by six," he said. "We'll have pizza or something on the way."

Allison opened her mouth, ready to give him a loud, positive no, but he slipped out the door and quickly shut it behind him. Amazed, she stared at the wooden panel, half expecting it to open again and for Nick to reappear. When he didn't, she quickly moved the few steps to the window and pulled the drapes aside.

She could see that he'd already jogged across the main road and was heading back to the Gallagher farmhouse.

Allison allowed the curtain to fall back into place, shutting out the sight of Nick Gallagher. What was she going to do now? The man was crazy! She had no intentions of going with him anywhere, and the sooner he realized that the better!

Back at the farmhouse, Nick was on his way to the den when he spotted Sam climbing the staircase.

"Going to bed already?" he called to his brother.

Sam turned to see Nick approaching the bottom of the staircase. "So you finally made it back. We were wondering what had happened to you."

Nick started up the stairs. "I went with Allison to help her put Ben to bed."

Sam grinned slyly. "Hmm. I wonder how she's

been managing to do that without you for the past three years?"

Nick shrugged and tried not to look sheepish. "I wouldn't know. How *has* she been doing it? Maybe you've been helping her?"

Sam laughed out loud. "Me? No. Allison is a nice girl and I like her, but I've never helped her put her son to bed."

Why did Nick suddenly feel so relieved? He knew Sam loved Olivia, and probably had even before she'd returned from Africa. Still, it would have bothered him to think that his brother and Allison might have been more than friends at one time. He didn't understand it. He'd just met the woman and he was already becoming proprietary about her. It was a scary thought.

"Then I wonder who has?" Nick asked before he could stop himself.

Sam clamped a hand on his brother's shoulder and gave it an affectionate shake. "My guess is you're the first."

Nick looked at him and grinned. "I'm not really interested. Just a little curious."

"Well, I could tell that right off," Sam said dryly.

The two men continued up the stairs. When they reached the landing, Nick asked, "Where's Olivia? Has she already gone to bed?"

Sam nodded. "She's still getting over a fever she

caught in Africa. I don't want her to wear herself out."

Nick studied his brother for a long moment. "You really love her, don't you?"

A wide, wondrous smile spread across Sam's face. "I really love her. Really, really love her."

"I'm glad," Nick told him. And he truly was. He wanted his brother to be happy. Although he'd be the first to admit that he didn't understand this devotion Sam had for Olivia. How could one woman have such an effect on a man? He'd certainly never experienced it before.

"But are you sure you want to step right into marriage?" Nick went on. "You've only been engaged a month."

Laughing, Sam slung his arm around his brother's shoulders. "When it's right, you don't have to think about it, Nick. You feel it. And you know."

Nick could hardly argue with that. He'd certainly never felt or known anything about love. At least not the kind of bond that rose above the physical. Yet, as the weight of Sam's arm lifted from his shoulder, he felt an odd sense of loss. Even though he and Sam had always been as different as night and day, they'd spent the bigger part of their lives together. While they were growing up Sam had understood Nick when their father hadn't even come close to understanding him. Now that his brother was getting married, Nick felt a strange sense of desertion.

"In case I haven't told you yet, I'm glad you made it home in time to be my best man," Sam said.

"Well," Nick attempted to joke, "somebody has to do it, and since the best man gets an extra kiss from the bride, what the hell?"

Grinning, Sam shoved him toward one of the bedroom doors. "Get out of here. I'll see you in the morning."

Allison recrossed her legs and pushed at the wilted lettuce with a plastic fork. Half of her lunch hour was over, but she'd barely gotten down a few bites.

She couldn't eat. Not when her stomach was clenched in knots. Thanks to Nick Gallagher, she thought grimly. Who did the man think he was? Did he think he could just force her into having a date with him? Just because he was some kind of drill sergeant didn't mean he could order her to go with him!

*It's not a date. It's simply going to get a Christmas tree,* she tried to tell herself.

"Allison, aren't you going to finish your lunch?" Gayle asked.

They were in the staff lounge, which also served as a lunchroom for the bank's employees. Allison looked across the table at her friend and co-worker.

"I think I've had all I want, Gayle. I'm just not hungry today."

"Oh, I hope you're not coming down with something. Especially with it being so close to Christmas."

Allison shook her head, then with a long sigh leaned back against the padded chair. "It's nothing serious. I just happen to have a problem I don't know how to deal with."

"So, what is the problem? Is it money?" Gayle asked.

"Who doesn't have money problems?" Allison replied, then grimaced. "No. It's a friend." Was Nick a friend? she suddenly asked herself. She barely knew him, so how could he be? "Well, maybe I should say an acquaintance. He wants to take me out to find a Christmas tree and—"

"He? There's a *he* in your life now? Allison! Why haven't you told me?"

Allison passed a weary hand across her forehead. "No, there is not a man in my life. This is—well, he's the son of a family I'm close to. And I—I just don't want to go with him. I've got to come up with some feasible excuse before tonight."

The petite brunette frowned back at her. "I suppose you want to come up with an excuse simply because he's male. Oh, Allison, when are you going to see that all men aren't like the one you were involved with?"

Other than Ella Gallagher, Gayle was the only person she'd ever talked to about her life back in Louisiana. As far as that went, Gayle was the only friend she had here in Fort Smith besides the Gallaghers.

Allison rose from her seat and crossed the room to a trash disposal. Gayle followed close on her heels. "I don't think they're all like Larry. But this one is—" Allison broke off, not really knowing how to describe Nick Gallagher. What was it about the man that set her on edge?

"Handsome?"

After dropping the paper plate in the disposal, Allison moved down the counter to a coffeemaker. "If you like the strong, tall, masculine type."

"I do! Tell me more," Gayle gushed as Allison filled her coffee cup.

"There's nothing to tell except that I don't want to go with him."

Gayle groaned. "Allison, I can't believe you! It's nearly Christmas. Where's your sense of adventure?"

Allison edged down the counter to an unoccupied corner of the room, with Gayle right behind her.

"My sense of adventure is taking Ben to the mall to have his picture taken on Santa's knee," Allison answered finally.

"Sounds exciting," the brunette said drolly.

Allison sipped her coffee, then looked at her friend. "No. It sounds safe. And safe is what I like best." Her expression was suddenly thoughtful. "Why don't you come over tonight, Gayle? With you there he would—"

Gayle was shaking her head before Allison could even finish. "No way. This is the closest thing to a date I've ever known of you having. I'm not going to be the one to spoil it."

Spoil it? She wanted a reprieve from it! "You're really some friend," Allison muttered.

Gayle giggled. "Of course I am. And who knows, someday you may be thankful that I *didn't* show up tonight."

Allison rolled her eyes. "*That* has to be the most ridiculous thing you've ever said to me."

Gayle merely laughed, but Allison didn't. She didn't find anything amusing about seeing Nick Gallagher again.

## Chapter 4

Nick reached over his mother's shoulder and dabbed his finger into the chocolate mixture she was stirring.

"Ouch! That stuff is hot!" Quickly, he licked the sticky goo off his fingers.

"This is going over the groom's cake, so keep your nasty ol' finger out of it," Ella said. She turned to whack him with the wooden spoon as his finger made another dive for the chocolate sauce.

Laughing, Nick pulled his hand back. "Okay, I'm going. You can put down your weapon."

Ella stood back and gave her son a second look. "Where are you going?" she asked curiously.

Smiling a bit craftily, Nick started toward the

door. "I'm taking Allison out to get a Christmas tree."

"And she agreed to go?"

"I didn't give her time not to," he replied wickedly.

Setting the saucepan aside, Ella hurried over to him while he slipped on a short leather bomber jacket. "Now, son, Allison isn't just any girl. You can't go—"

Nick held up his hand before his mother could give him a list of warnings. "Mom, I'm not going to drag her down a road of decadence. We're merely going to get a Christmas tree."

She gave him a long, pointed look, one that hadn't changed since he'd turned thirteen and she'd caught him trying to smoke one of his father's cigarettes. "Allison doesn't have the money to buy an expensive spruce. Why not wait and cut one in the woods?"

"Dad and Sam have cleared every cedar off these five hundred acres, and I'm not fond of trespassing on someone else's property. Besides, I intend to buy the tree for her."

Ella shook her head. "She has pride, Nick."

Nick leaned forward and kissed his mother's cheek. "Don't worry, Mom. I'll be so slippery about it, she'll think she's done me a favor by allowing me to buy it."

"She's not a fluffhead, Nicholas, so don't you try to treat her like one."

Nick laughed. "For Pete's sake, Mom, you are a mother hen where she's concerned, aren't you?"

Ella shrugged. "Somebody needs to look after her. The poor darling is so young, and she's been through so much."

Nick would have liked to ask his mother to explain, but before he could, she went on, "Besides, I thought you would go with Sam and your father tonight. Why didn't you?"

Nick fastened the ends of his jacket together and pulled the zipper midway up his chest. "I'm not into farmer-stockmen meetings."

"I know. But S.T. rarely ever gets to be with you."

"Sam will be a lot better company for him than I would have been. I don't know anything about farming anymore."

Ella scowled. "Don't be ridiculous. Just because you've been in the army for six years doesn't mean you've forgotten what you learned here on the farm. Anyway, it would have been nice for the three of you to have had a night out together. Especially since Sam is getting married tomorrow night."

How could Nick explain to his mother that when it came down to him, Sam and their father, Nick always came away feeling like an outsider? He couldn't tell her that. Not without sounding jealous or resentful.

"Well, I've already told Allison to expect me. And what man in his right mind would want to spend an evening with two farmers instead of a beautiful woman?" He did his best to joke.

Laughing, Ella shooed him toward the door. "All right. You've made your point. Tell Allison hello and that we'll be expecting her early tomorrow evening."

With a grin and a quick salute, Nick left his mother and drove the short distance to the old Lee place.

Since his arrival yesterday, the weather had taken a turn for the worse. The temperature had dropped twenty degrees and the light mist that had started falling earlier that afternoon was on the verge of turning into snow.

He was raising his hand to knock for the third time when she came to the door. Her red hair was flying loose about her face and shoulders, and water was splotched across the front of her purple blouse. She was the sexiest thing he could ever remember seeing.

"Hello," he said.

As soon as Allison had heard the knock on the door, her heart had catapulted into a gallop. Now that she could see his tall, lean body standing on the other side of the screen door, the same fevered pace continued.

"Hello," she replied.

She stood there without saying more. Nick gestured toward the door.

"May I come in?"

How could she refuse? All day long she'd tried to

think of a good reason to put him back on the road to the Gallagher place, but she'd failed to come up with even one. It was a cinch that she wasn't going to think of something in a matter of a few seconds.

"Of course," she said, then opened the door wide enough for him to enter.

"You didn't forget I'd be here, did you?" he asked once he was standing in the middle of the room.

Allison took her time making sure the door was tightly closed before she turned around to face him. "Er…no. I didn't forget."

Nick glanced quickly around the room. It was clean, but cluttered; mostly with toys, newspapers and books. A fire was going in the fireplace. From the looks of it, she'd started it only a few minutes ago. The house seemed even chillier tonight than it had last night. He could feel a cold draft against his legs. More than likely it was coming from the old paned windows on the north wall.

"That's good," he said. "Where's Ben?"

She ran a hand over her tousled hair, then motioned for Nick to take a seat on the couch. "I've just gotten him out of the tub. That's why I'm so wet. Er—uh—it won't take a minute for me to dress him."

Nick nodded. "Sure. Go ahead. We have plenty of time."

*Plenty of time.* Was Nick going to try to make this into a whole evening affair? Groaning to herself, she hurried out of the room.

She found Ben using her bed as a trampoline. She hauled him down from the middle of the mattress and managed to calm him long enough to dress him in jeans and a thick sweatshirt. But the moment she released him he dashed out of the room.

With Benjamin out of the way, Allison decided she'd better do something about her own appearance. She moved over to a dresser to grab the hairbrush, but the image staring back at her caused her hand to pause in midair.

She looked horrible! Her face was pale and lined with fatigue. Her hair resembled a limp dishrag. Oh, well, what did it matter? She didn't want to impress Nick. She wanted to get rid of him. In a nice, but final way.

Out in the living room Nick was a bit surprised as Benjamin sidled up against his knee. The boy was carrying Kathleen's old stuffed dog, and he looked at Nick with big, curious eyes.

"Hi," Nick said with a grin. "Do you remember my name?"

Benjamin nodded. "Nick."

"That's right. And yours is Ben, isn't it?"

Benjamin nodded with the same aplomb he'd used the first time.

"I see you still like Buddy. Is he a pretty good dog?" Nick asked.

"Pretty good," Ben repeated, then climbed up beside Nick on the couch.

An indulgent smile creased Nick's face as he looked down at the boy's red head. He liked small children, although he rarely had the chance to be around them. "What have you asked Santa Claus to bring you this year?" Nick asked him.

"A tractor."

Nick should have known. The boy had probably watched Sam plowing the fields around the house and been impressed by the huge machines. As a child Nick had been impressed, too. Although as he'd grown older he began to wonder what there was to like about turning the soil. Especially when the weather was dry and the dust so thick you could hardly see ten feet in front of you. But Nick had always wanted to measure up to Sam, and Sam had taken to farming like a duck to water.

Turning his thoughts back to the moment, he looked at Benjamin. "Well, if you've been a good boy I'm sure Santa will bring you a tractor."

Benjamin pushed a finger at Buddy's black nose, then gave the tail a tug. "Yep, he will."

Nick laughed to himself. Benjamin might be short on words, but he got the point over with the few he did use.

Moments later, Allison entered the room, surprised to see her son had already become comfortable with Nick. Usually it took him several meetings to warm up to people, and even then he was choosy about whom he liked and didn't like.

"Sorry to keep you waiting. I had to stop for milk and bread on the way home, and then the pilot light on the hot-water heater had gone out and the water was too cold for Ben's bath—" She broke off, embarrassed. This man didn't care about her mundane problems.

Nick studied her flushed cheeks and hesitant smile. "Don't apologize, Allison. I'm not going to."

"Not going to what? Apologize?" she asked, her expression quizzical.

He nodded as a grin spread over his face. "For railroading you into this outing. I know you don't want to go."

Allison's already pink cheeks turned a deep crimson. "I have a mouth and I know how to use it. If I didn't want to go, I'd tell you so."

His thick dark brows arched with wry speculation. "Oh. Then you *do* want to go. I'm glad I was wrong."

Allison didn't know what kept her from groaning aloud. How had she managed to back herself into that? Now he really was going to believe she wanted to go. *From now on, Allison, say as little as possible and keep your thoughts to yourself.*

Five minutes later they were driving across Gallagher farmland. It had been dark for some time and, on the not-too-distant horizon, the lights of Fort Smith lighted up the sky.

Since they'd left the house, Allison had stuck

to her own advice and said very little. It was safer that way.

"I would have brought my car tonight, but since we're getting a tree, I decided Sam's pickup would be more appropriate," Nick explained. "I hope you don't mind."

She looked at him. However, in the darkness of the cab she could only make out the faint line of his profile. "Why should I mind?"

Nick laughed. "He lets Jake and Leo ride around with him. You'll probably be picking dog hairs off of you for a week."

"A few dog hairs won't bother me or Ben," she assured him. "Besides, you've seen my car. It's far more worn than this truck."

Nick glanced over at her, quickly taking in her jeans and sweater. Last night she'd admitted that she wouldn't be able to dress up for Sam's wedding. Yet she hadn't sounded sorry for herself then or now. It was more than obvious that Allison Lee was a woman who didn't have or expect to have luxuries of any kind. Her quiet pride made him want to give to her and keep on giving. Anything and everything she would accept from him.

"I hope you're both hungry," he said, putting his thoughts aside. "Is Benjamin old enough to eat pizza?"

"He loves pizza. But you hardly have to feed us. We can eat sandwiches when we get back home."

"I know I don't *have* to feed you. I want to feed you. Ben here is a growing boy. He needs groceries in his belly."

Reaching over, Nick patted the child's abdomen. Benjamin giggled loudly, then patted himself in the exact spot Nick had.

"Belly," he repeated with another giggle.

Nick chuckled. Allison rolled her eyes, though inside she was smiling, too.

"Do you live on the army base?" she asked Nick. "Or do you have a civilian house?"

He was surprised that she was asking him something personal. He knew she'd been trying her best to keep him at a distance. "I live on the base," he answered.

"I was just wondering. I guess you're hardly ever around children?"

"Not too often. Although some of the fresh recruits are more like children than men."

Allison nervously fingered the hem of her purple sweater. "Well, it probably takes some of them longer to adapt to army life than others."

"You're right. It either makes them or breaks them."

Obviously it hadn't broken Sergeant Nick Gallagher, she silently mused, her eyes gliding over his broad shoulders, the strong line of his jaw and the tough looking hands holding the steering wheel.

Throughout the day, Allison had told herself she

wasn't the least bit curious about Nick Gallagher. But now that she was actually with him, she found herself wondering about the man in spite of herself.

What had he been like in the beginning when he'd been a young recruit? she wondered. Why had he entered the military instead of becoming a farmer like his father and brother? Allison was surprised at just how much she longed to ask him.

"What made you want to be a soldier?"

Nick shrugged, then gave her a twisted grin. "I guess I liked the tough, macho image."

"You didn't like farming?"

She saw his eyes narrow a fraction before he turned them back on the road. "I was always better at fighting than I was at farming."

She didn't comment on that and Nick was glad. He didn't like talking about himself. At least not in a serious way. He didn't want to think too much about the course his life had taken. It was easier just to accept it and go on.

"Do you like your job?" he asked her.

"It's probably as good as I'll get without furthering my education," she said.

"Would you like to go to college?"

Allison lowered her eyes as the memory of Larry and her college days flashed through her mind. "I was on my second year, but I—things got sidetracked."

He supposed she was referring to having Benjamin. What had happened? he wondered. Was the child's father still in their lives? It didn't seem so. From the looks of things, Allison Lee was doing her best to take care of herself and her son without any outside help. So where was the rest of her family?

"My father wanted me to go to college," Nick said, surprised that his wondering about her was making him open up in ways he usually didn't. "I disappointed him by entering the military."

There was an odd inflection in his voice that made Allison lift her head and look at him. She could have sworn there had been a bit of sadness behind his words. Or maybe it had been regret. She couldn't tell exactly. Either way, she felt herself drawn to him because of it.

"I hardly think so. S.T. seems very proud of you."

Nick kept his mocking snort to himself. He didn't want to give Allison the impression that he was at odds with his father, because actually he wasn't at odds with him. It was just that sometimes Nick had trouble accepting that his father looked upon him as second best.

"Maybe," he said.

Maybe? What an odd response, she thought. Did Nick actually think his father wasn't proud of him? Allison couldn't imagine it. During the time she'd known the Gallaghers, S.T. had often mentioned Nick and had always spoken of him with high regard.

Perhaps she should tell him so, Allison silently

mused. Then she quickly decided against it. Nick's relationship with his family was none of her business. She'd had enough problems with her own father to know better than to try to counsel someone else about theirs.

Nick drove them to a popular pizza place on Rogers Avenue. It was filled to capacity with evening diners. No doubt most of them were out tonight doing their Christmas shopping, Allison thought.

They managed to find a booth at the back of the room. It was only a moment or two before a waitress came to take their order. When the young woman returned with their drinks and a booster seat for Benjamin, Nick took the latter from the waitress and placed it near him.

Allison looked doubtfully from her son to Nick. "You're taking a big chance," she told Nick. "You might be leaving here with tomato sauce all over your shirt."

And it was a nice, expensive shirt, too, she decided. She could tell just by looking at the heavy black cotton and the detailed stitching. She could also see that it fit his broad shoulders perfectly and complimented his dark hair and swarthy skin. But the attractive side of Nick Gallagher was something she was trying her best not to notice tonight. So far she was failing miserably.

"A little tomato sauce never hurt anybody," he

assured her, plopping Ben into the small seat before Allison could say more.

"Do you come home every Christmas?" she asked, taking a sip of her coffee.

He nodded. "Always. Sometimes I may have to leave a few days early or arrive a few days late. But I'm always home for Christmas."

A wan smile touched her lips. "I can see why. You have a wonderful family."

Nick handed Ben his milk, helping him with the straw before turning his attention back to Allison. "And what about you? Do you have a big, rowdy family back in Louisiana?"

Allison's features were suddenly drawn and he watched a silent struggle going on behind them before she lifted her eyes back up to him. "No. I don't have a large family. I'm an only child. My mother died from a rare blood disorder when I was very small. My father still lives in Monroe—but I rarely ever see him."

From the sound of her voice, she didn't want to see him, either, Nick realized. The fact surprised him, because Allison seemed such a family-oriented person.

Nick reached for his coffee cup. "I can't imagine life without my family, although I don't get to see them that often anymore. I guess just knowing they're here is like an anchor to me."

At that moment, Benjamin spotted a small Christmas tree displayed in a front window of the restaurant. It was decorated with silver tinsel, bright red balls and a countless number of twinkling lights.

"Christmas tree!" Benjamin said, pointing excitedly at the object. All the wonder and excitement of Christmas was shining in his wide eyes. Seeing the child's innocent joy had Nick remembering his own Christmases as a small boy. He'd almost forgotten how everything had seemed so magical and bright back then.

"As soon as we eat," Nick told him, "we're going to go find one for you and your mother. Okay?"

Benjamin giggled at the prospect. "Okay!"

"I think Ben was too small to remember last Christmas," Allison told Nick. "But he's making up for it this year."

Nick leaned back comfortably against the vinyl seat, then impulsively reached over to ruffle Benjamin's bright red hair. "Seeing Ben reminds me how it was to be a child at Christmas. Dad would always load us up in the pickup and we'd jostle over the pasture until we reached the wooded part of our land. That's when the fun and the arguing began over which tree to cut. Kathleen always wanted a pine tree and Sam wanted one that would reach the ceiling."

Allison laughed softly. "That would have to be quite a tree, since the ceilings are so high in your family's house. What kind of tree did you want?"

Nick shrugged. "It never really mattered that

much to me as long as I got to help chop it down. And put the icicles on it. That was the special job my mother gave to me."

Allison absently traced the rim of her coffee cup with her fingertip. "My fondest memories of Christmas as a child were those times we visited Grandmother Lee. We always helped her put up the tree and decorate it with strings of popcorn and cranberries. She had a set of wooden figures my grandfather had carved from hickory and hand painted. I was fascinated by them and Grandmother let me choose the exact places to hang them."

Nick watched a lovely glow spread over Allison's face as she talked of the happier times in her life, and he decided it was the way she should always look—with a warm joy in her eyes, a soft smile curving her lips. "I wonder why I never saw you over at your grandmother's?" he asked.

"Maybe you did, but just don't remember me."

"I would have remembered," he said, his eyes glinting as they traveled over her face.

She looked away from him and drew in a long breath. "Well, we stopped coming after Mother died. I had just turned seven at the time. At that age you wouldn't have been interested in a girl."

"Probably," he agreed, watching a sad shadow flicker across her face. "So why didn't you come back? Doesn't your father ever come up to see Martha? She is his mother, isn't she?"

Allison shook her head. "As far as Clifford Lee is concerned he doesn't have any family. He didn't want any after mother died, you see."

Nick was beginning to see a lot of things. Except for one. How had Allison survived as well as she had without any parents or loved ones to help her?

After they'd finished their pizza, Nick drove them to a big lot filled with cut Christmas trees. Before they climbed out of the truck to choose one, Allison carefully bundled Benjamin in his coat, hood and mittens, then donned her own coat.

"This isn't quite like cutting your own," Nick told her as they walked through the maze of evergreen trees, "but the end result is just as good."

"Trees! Big trees!" Benjamin exclaimed, tugging on his mother's hand and pointing toward several tall Colorado blue spruces standing directly in front of them.

"Yes, Ben. They are big," Allison told him. "Too big for us," she added, thinking of the few meager bills she had left in her wallet. "We need something smaller. Santa likes small trees as well as he does big ones."

Nick bent down and picked Benjamin up so the boy could get a better look around him. "I'm sure your mother is right," Nick said, "but we like big trees, don't we, Ben?"

"Yeah! Big trees! Get a big tree, Mommy!"

Allison cast Nick an irritated look. "Gee, thanks. You really know how to deal with children."

"Can I help you folks find a tree?"

Nick and Allison both looked over their shoulder to see a teenage boy bundled in a heavy coat and stocking cap.

"Sorry I was busy when you first drove up," he said. "My helper called in sick tonight."

"No hurry," Nick assured him. "After all, this is Christmas and picking out a tree is a special thing. We don't want to get it over with too quickly."

"That's right," the teenager agreed, obviously relieved to find Nick wasn't going to be a demanding customer. He pushed at the glasses on his nose. "Did you have a certain tree in mind?"

Nick nodded, then looked at Ben, who was snuggling against his shoulder. The child deserved and needed a father that would love him. Nick couldn't very well be his father, but at least he could make Ben's Christmas a bit brighter by giving him a tree to remember.

"We want a big one. A big blue spruce."

"Uh, Nick, I—" Allison was suddenly stammering and she felt her cheeks burn as Nick and the salesboy looked at her. "We don't want a big one. We want a little one, remember?"

"Excuse us a minute, will you," Nick told the teen, then taking Allison by the arm, he pulled her to the side.

"Nick, I hate to be a Scrooge about this, but—"

"Allison, don't worry about cost. I'm buying the tree, so please let me buy what I think is best."

Nick watched her eyes widen and her mouth drop open. He could see she was going to argue. The fact merely amused him.

"You're buying? Not on your life! I came on this outing tonight because I—well, just because. But that doesn't give you the right to buy me a Christmas tree."

Smiling patiently at her, he bent his head closer to her ear. "This is not a bribe for sexual favors, Allison. It's more like a chance to get myself in the good graces of my soon-to-be sister-in-law."

"Olivia?" she asked quizzically, even though her mind was still trying to digest that part about the sexual favors.

"Yes, Olivia. The sales from these trees goes to the underprivileged children in this area. So I wouldn't feel right if I didn't buy the most expensive one they have. Olivia would expect nothing less from me."

"So you're doing this for Olivia?" she asked, still skeptical.

Nick looked at the child tucked in the crook of his left arm, then felt his heart melt a bit as Ben smiled back at him. "Uh—yes. And you could also say for my conscience. I'd hate to think some little guy like Ben might not get a toy for Christmas."

Put like that, what could she say? Allison asked herself. "Well, I guess it's all right then."

"Of course it's all right," Nick said brightly as he led her back to the waiting salesboy. "This is Christmas. The time for giving."

"Did you decide what you'd like?" the teen asked, rubbing his hands together to ward off the cold.

"We have," Nick told him. "The biggest Colorado blue spruce you can find in the bunch."

## Chapter 5

"It's a big tree, Mommy," Ben said on the way home.

The boy was looking out the back windshield at the mound of green branches.

"It sure is, honey," Allison said, and so was the price, she thought ruefully. But Nick's gift would make Ben's Christmas special—she had to look at it that way.

"Think we can get it into the house?" Nick asked him.

Ben nodded. "Yep. And it's big enough for Santa to put a tractor under."

Nick laughed. "That's right. There might even be

enough room left for him to leave Mommy something, too."

Allison wasn't going to hold her breath waiting for that something to come, but she didn't say so aloud. She didn't want anything to spoil the mystery and excitement of Ben's Christmas.

*As long as you believe in Santa, Allison, there will always be a Santa.* The words of her mother ran through Allison's mind, bringing with them a bittersweet ache. During the time her mother had been alive, Allison had believed in Santa and all the special magic of Christmas. But after her death, the holidays had become just one more day for Allison.

The thought had her reaching out and snuggling Benjamin closer to her side. She never wanted things to be like that for her son.

Nick glanced over at her. "What do you want for Christmas, Allison?"

She shook her head. "Having Ben is enough for me."

She loved her son very much, Nick could see. Did that mean she'd loved his father just as much? Nick wondered. Or maybe he shouldn't have used the past tense. Maybe she still loved the man. The very idea turned Nick cold, but even so, he knew he had to find out.


"What's happened to the living room? It's shrunk!" Allison exclaimed a few minutes later, after she and Nick had tugged the tree into the house.

"It is big, isn't it?" Nick commented as he eyed the top of the spruce. It was bent against the ceiling and it wasn't even on the stand yet.

"It's pretty, Mommy! Santa Claus will like it!" Benjamin said with a happy squeal.

Nick couldn't help but laugh at the child's enthusiasm. "He'll like it as long as it doesn't fall on his head," he told Ben.

Allison found a hacksaw and Nick cut the bottom of the trunk two times before the tree would fit between the floor and the ceiling. Once it was finally standing upright and secure, Allison decided she wanted it placed in front of the windows.

Carefully, Nick scooted it over to the chosen spot. "Now," he said, stepping back to admire his handiwork. "Do you have decorations?"

Not enough for a tree that size, she thought. But enough to make do. "My grandmother's ornaments are in the attic. It won't take me a minute to find them."

She turned to leave the room, with Ben close behind her. Nick followed even though he hadn't been invited. "Let me get them for you," he offered. "It's dark up there."

Allison could feel him close behind her, and suddenly she was remembering last night and how he'd stood beside her in the darkness while she'd put her son to bed. Something about him had tugged at her then, and that same something was tugging at her now.

"The opening in the ceiling is pretty small. It might be better if I do it. But you could keep an eye on Benjamin for me while I go after a chair and flashlight."

When she returned, she positioned the chair beneath the trapdoor in the ceiling and handed him the flashlight. "If you'll hold this, I'll see if I can open this door. In the summer when the humidity is high, it warps and sticks. But it should open now."

Nick held the light on the small trapdoor while Allison unfastened the hook, then swung the door wide. The movement caused dust to pour from the ceiling. It covered Allison's hair and filled her mouth and nostrils.

"Allison, maybe I'd better do this," Nick said, as she coughed and spluttered.

"No, I'm okay. Just give my foot a little boost."

Nick gave Benjamin the job of holding the flashlight. However, as soon as Nick reached for Allison's foot, the child decided to make a game of whirling the light in dizzying circles.

In the darkness his hands groped, then latched around the calf of her leg. The unexpected touch of his hands made Allison jerk and nearly topple over on him. "I said my foot, Nick!"

"I know. Don't kick me. I'm headed in that direction," he said, while Benjamin continued to giggle and flash the light everywhere but on the two adults.

Allison held her breath as his hands gently felt their way downward. When his warm fingers finally curled around her ankle the air whooshed from her lungs.

"Ready?" he asked.

Ready? Ready for what? She'd almost forgotten what she was supposed to be doing. "Uh—yes, okay," she told him, grabbing on to the edges of the opening in the ceiling.

Nick gave a little lift and Allison did her best to wriggle up and through the small opening. Any other time, it was a snap for her to climb up into the attic, but having Nick around must have thrown her off-kilter. Now she found herself hanging in limbo, unable to pull herself up or lower herself back to the chair.

"Can you make it now?" he called to her dangling legs.

Her muffled voice frantically shouted down to him. "No! Nick, do something! I think I'm stuck!"

"Don't worry. Here, let me—"

The next thing Allison knew, two male hands were cupping her bottom, pushing her upward. Before she realized what was happening, she landed on the floor of the attic with a hard thud.

"Allison? Allison, are you all right?"

Nick took the light from Ben and pointed the beam into the hole in the ceiling. It was a long time before her face peered over the edge. When it did, her expression was indignant.

"I guess my hind end was the only thing you could manage to get a hold of," she said tersely.

Nick shrugged and tried not to laugh at her outraged expression. "It just seemed like the natural thing to do."

"Handling women's bottoms comes naturally to you, does it?"

Was she really angry? Surely not. He couldn't imagine anyone being that proper! "Er, no. Well, I mean it is a natural male instinct. Uh—but one I don't give in to—very often."

"I'm sure," she muttered more to herself than to him.

"You didn't want me to let you fall, did you?" he asked. Unable to stop himself, he grinned up at her.

Part of her wanted to smile back at him, while the wary, distrustful part of her wanted to be cross with him. In spite of herself she was beginning to like Nick Gallagher, but she was so afraid he would turn out to be just like most other men, out only for their own physical pleasure.

That's crazy, Allison, she told herself. Nick is only here to help you with a Christmas tree. That little fondle on the bottom was nothing to him but a helping hand. And if you make a big deal out of it he's going to think you're crazy.

Taking a bracing breath, she smiled back at him. "No. I guess not."

"Good. I knew you couldn't think I was that wicked."

She didn't think Nick Gallagher was wicked. She knew he was!

Taking the flashlight from his outstretched hand, Allison went to find the Christmas decorations. Yet even the sound of mice scampering across the attic floor couldn't pull her mind away from the man waiting for her down below. Damn him anyway, she thought. Why did he have to be so tempting? So threatening to her peace of mind?

After a moment of prowling around in the cold, cramped attic, Allison found what she was looking for and handed the box down to Nick. While he was setting it aside, Allison swung her legs over the edge of the opening to lower herself down. Too late, she noticed that Ben was pushing the chair down the hallway.

"Nick!"

The cry of his name had him turning blindly and reaching for her. She fell hard against him, the impact of her weight causing him to stagger against the wall.

By the time Allison's senses had righted themselves, she realized Nick had caught her and now the front of her body was sliding slowly, inch by inch, down the front of his.

"Allison, my God, you could have…" His words trailed away as fear for her was replaced by something altogether different. He could feel her breasts pushing impudently against his chest, her hips pressing against his.

"Allison."

The sound of her name on his breath was almost as erotic as finding herself thrust up against him. He felt warm and solid. So powerful, and so deliciously male. She'd almost forgotten what it felt like to be held by a man. In fact, she'd tried to make herself forget, but Nick was bringing it all back, making her fingers curl unwittingly over his shoulders.

"Allison?" His hands moved against her back, drawing her a fraction closer.

It was the question in his hands, and not the one in his voice that brought her back to her senses. What was she doing? she wondered desperately. She had to get out of his arms! She had to stop the hot, erotic feelings that were burgeoning inside of her!

With all the willpower she could muster, she shifted out of his warm embrace and turned her back to him. "Nick, I…" Not knowing what to say, she stopped and drew in a shaky breath.

Straightening away from the wall, Nick took a step toward her. Had those few seconds he'd held her shaken her as much as it had him? he wondered.

"You could have hurt yourself," he finally said,

when it was obvious she wasn't going to say anything else.

In more ways than one, Allison silently groaned. Determined to make light of the moment, she squared her shoulders and turned back to him.

"I guess clumsy should be my middle name. Thank you for catching me. This is probably the most dangerous tree trimming you've ever been to. Imagine what all your recruits would say if they were told their sergeant had been squashed to death by a woman falling out of an attic."

She *had* been shaken, Nick decided, as his gaze caught the faint quiver of her lower lip. She was just determined not to let him know it.

"They'd probably all say what a way to go," he said, still watching her thoughtfully.

Reaching for the box, she forced herself to laugh. "I think you're full of nonsense."

Right now he was full of her, Nick thought. Full of the sight, the smell, the feel of her. More than anything he wanted to take her back into his arms, taste her full lips, feel her breath on his cheek as she sighed in surrender.

"Mommy! Come on," Ben called as he scampered back down the hall to the two adults. "Let's make a Christmas tree!"

The child's voice broke into the awkward silence, suddenly reminding Nick why he was here in Allison's house in the first place. He was here simply to help her with a tree, to help her celebrate the holidays a little bit. Nothing more than that.

It would be a big mistake to start getting ideas about making love to Allison Lee, he firmly told himself. Obviously she wasn't the kind who took relationships lightly. Hell, from what Sam had said, she didn't have relationships, period. Not physical, or any other kind. And Nick certainly wasn't ready to get serious about a woman. Not even one that turned his mind to mush and sent his libido into overdrive. So why did he suddenly feel so serious?

Nick carried the box to the living room and placed it in the middle of the floor. Allison kneeled beside him and waited eagerly while he broke the twine tied around it.

"Grandmother said she hadn't used these in several years. I don't know what we'll find," she told him.

"Let's see," Nick said, lifting the lid.

Allison reached in and began to dig through the decorations. She found a single silver garland, two strings of lights, a handful of icicles, a box of glass ornaments and the carved wooden ornaments her grandfather had made many years ago. There were six of them in all, each one wrapped separately in newspaper—a Santa, a reindeer, two toy soldiers, an angel and a snowman.

Nick watched Allison lovingly inspect each one,

then carefully lay them out with the rest of the things. It was plain that the ornaments reminded her of a more pleasant time in her life. He was glad about that. But it was also painfully obvious that there weren't nearly enough of them to cover the huge tree.

"Well," she said, looking up at him. "Shall we plug in the lights and see if they work?"

"Uh—Allison, I think we're going to need more decorations. Let's run over to the mall. I'll buy," he added quickly, in case she was worried about the expense.

Allison shook her head. "No! You've already bought the tree."

"That doesn't matter. Come on, put Ben's coat on and let's go before the stores close."

"I said no, Nick." She turned her back on him and carried the lights over to the nearest electrical outlet.

"But, Allison, I—"

She whirled back around. "Look, Nick, I'm not like you. I don't just run out and buy things on a whim. Besides, I want to use *these* decorations."

He threw up his hands. "But it's Christmas. That's when a person is supposed to buy," he reasoned, still not understanding why she was being so adamant about this.

Sighing, she bent down and plugged in one of the strings of lights. As they blinked to life, Allison glanced back up at him. "That's not what Christmas is about, Nick."

"It's about giving gifts, isn't it? And that's what I'm trying to do. If you'd let me," he added.

"I know you're trying to be helpful," she said, straightening up. "But by the time we drove back into town and shopped for decorations, Ben would be sound asleep. I want him to enjoy decorating the tree tonight before his bedtime."

Nick looked over at the child who was staring up at the tree with wide, wondrous eyes. "I guess you think I'm thoughtless and impulsive," he said after a moment.

"No."

The guarded sound in her voice had his brows inching upward. "You don't sound too sure about that."

She laughed softly. "I think you're a typical bachelor. One who's used to being impulsive and enjoying himself just for the moment."

Maybe sometimes he was guilty of that, he thought a bit ruefully. But not now. He wasn't out for just a laugh or two. Giving to her and Benjamin was something that would stay with him long after Christmas passed. In fact, he somehow knew this time spent with her and her son was something he'd never forget. But how could he tell her that without sounding like some sort of slick charmer?

"That isn't entirely a bad thing, is it? People are supposed to enjoy living," he said, surprised at how important her opinion was to him.

"Yes. I know. It's just that I'm a more practical person," she told him, bending down to plug in the second string of lights.

She was more than practical, he thought. In fact, he doubted Allison Lee ever lived for just the thrill of the moment. He'd never seen anyone so young be so serious-minded. But then, he supposed, the responsibility of raising a child by herself had made her that way.

"Well, you're right anyway," Nick said after a moment. "Santa will still come no matter how many ornaments are on the tree." As he turned and winked at Benjamin, another thought struck him. "Allison, we could make some things to put on the tree. Do you have any popcorn or cranberries?"

Her expression brightened as she saw where his thoughts were leading this time. "Yes, I do. We can use them to make garlands! Why didn't I think of that earlier? I remember in school we used to make stars from aluminum foil, too. We could make a big one for the top."

Nick was relieved to see he was on the right track with her this time. "Now you're talking! Let's get to work," he said, rubbing his hands together with eager anticipation.

Bending down beside Allison, he began to help her untangle the string of lights. "Have I redeemed myself now?" he asked her after a moment.

Allison glanced up at his face, now so very close

to hers. There was a smile on his lips, an earnest look in his smoky blue eyes. Even though she tried, she couldn't stop herself from smiling shyly back at him.

"Don't be silly. You don't have to redeem yourself to me. We're just friends."

Just friends. Nick was stunned as the simple words rolled over in his mind. He didn't want the two of them to be just friends. He wanted them to be more. Much more. What was happening to him? he wondered. This woman had done something to him from the first moment he'd seen her. And though he'd never been one to believe in love at first sight, he was afraid he was feeling something damn near to it.

Nick's eyes slipped over her face, and the warmth and beauty he saw there sent an unexplained emotion sweeping over him. "Allison, I—"

"Mommy! Look at the lights!"

Benjamin's excited cry had Allison releasing a long, tense breath. She looked down at the lights at their feet, to see they were flashing on and off. She hadn't even noticed, she realized with a start. Her mind had been far away, wondering what it would be like to be the recipient of Nick Gallagher's lovemaking.

"I think they're supposed to do that, sport," Nick told the boy.

Allison quickly unplugged them and suggested they carry the lights over to the tree and finish untangling them there.

Nick knew the moment between him and Allison was gone. But maybe that was for the best, he thought. Even now, he wasn't sure what he'd been about to say to her. He only knew that a warm, wonderful feeling had taken hold of him and he wanted her to share in it. But the night wasn't over, he reminded himself. It was far from over.

For the next half hour the three of them decorated the blue spruce with the decorations they'd found in the attic, and in Ben's words, made a Christmas tree. Allison gave Ben the task of hanging ornaments on the bottom branches, while Nick worked on the tallest ones. However, when they got to the icicles, Allison decided it would be best to put them on after the popcorn-and-cranberry garland.

"Santa is going to see this tree the minute his sleigh flies over the river," Nick told Ben as they all three admired the tree that was beginning to sparkle in spite of the meager decorations.

Ben's eyes somehow grew even wider. "Can reindeer really fly?" he asked Nick.

Nick squatted down to the child's level. "Well, I'm not sure about all reindeer, Ben. But Santa has special reindeer."

"Why does he?"

Allison looked down on the two of them and felt something stir in her breast. Nick had confessed he didn't know much about small children, but still he seemed to know exactly what to say and do with Ben. Her son was completely taken with the man.

"Well," Nick said, "Santa has little boys and girls all over the world waiting for him to bring them a toy, so he needs the reindeer to fly him around in a hurry."

Ben nodded as though he accepted Nick's explanation. "Mommy says he comes down the chimney. But I told her he'd get burnt."

Nick cut his eyes up to Allison. "Smart kid."

"Very logical," she said with a smile.

"Like his mother?"

"I try to be."

Nick wondered what she meant by that, but it was impossible to read exactly what was in her expression. Turning his attention back to Ben, he said, "I'll bet your mommy will let the fire go out the night Santa comes. Then we won't have to worry about him getting burnt."

Nick's suggestion seemed to please Benjamin. With a happy laugh he went back to the tree, standing as close to it as possible without touching the branches.

Allison had never seen her son so absorbed or excited over anything, and just seeing him so happy lifted her own spirits. "I think I'd better go pop the popcorn or we'll never get it strung. Would you two like a cookie break?"

For an answer, Benjamin raced to the kitchen

ahead of the two adults. Nick slowly rose up to his full height.

"I could use some coffee if you have it," Nick said.

"I do. It will only take a few minutes to make."

"I'll make it while you start the popcorn," he said, following her out of the room.

The kitchen was small, a bit cluttered, but basically clean. While Benjamin climbed up on a chair at the table, Nick joined Allison at the counter.

She quickly showed him where the coffee makings were. While he put them together, she went to work measuring popcorn and oil into a heavy pot.

"Benjamin and I have been baking Christmas cookies this past week. We're going to take some of them to the nursing home where Grandmother stays."

With the coffee dripping, Nick leaned casually against the cabinets and watched her work.

"That's nice. But how do you have the time?"

She laughed softly at his question. "I let something else go. Can't you tell by looking?" she asked, motioning with her hand.

"The kitchen looks fine to me."

She shot him a look of wry disbelief. "That coming from a drill sergeant? You'd put your soldiers on permanent guard duty if you found their barracks in this shape, I'll bet."

Smiling, he folded his arms across his chest. It was a joy to watch her work. She moved with an unconscious grace that constantly reminded him that she was a woman. The purple cable-knit sweater she was wearing over a pair of blue jeans was anything but glamorous. But something about the way she looked in it was just as sexy as if she'd been in a clingy dress and high heels.

"But we're not in a military barrack now," he pointed out. "We're in a home. And I like the way yours is. Nice and lived-in."

Laughing once again, she quickly filled a plate with sugar cookies. "Well, you got the lived-in part right."

After carrying the cookies to the table, she went to pour Benjamin a glass of milk. By then the popcorn had started to pop. Nick went over to the stove and gave the pot a shake.

"Does Martha resent being in a nursing home?" Nick asked.

With Benjamin taken care of, Allison joined him at the stove. "Not really. Of course, who wouldn't like to stay young and do all the things they've always done? But Grandmother understands that she has limitations now that she's in her nineties. In fact, I begged her to live with me, but she wouldn't have any part of it. She doesn't want to be a burden."

Nick nodded. "That's not hard to understand. No one wants to feel like they're a burden."

The popcorn had quit popping. Allison reached around Nick to move the pot from the burner. Nick felt her arm brush his side and realized he was probably in the way. Even so, he didn't move. He wasn't going to pass up any chance to have her by his side.

"Actually, Grandmother has lots of friends at the home. She and several of the other ladies work on their quilting together. You'd be surprised at how well she can still sew just by feeling rather than seeing."

"She must be an inspiration to you."

Her green eyes cut up to his. "Yes. She is. She's been alone for a long time and survived. I can, too."

No doubt Allison could survive, Nick thought. But was that all she wanted from life? Just to survive?

Allison felt his shoulder touching hers and knew that he was too close. That she was *letting* him get too close. Other than Sam who was kind enough to bring her firewood or drop by to see if she needed anything fixed, she hadn't invited a man into this house. Especially not one like Sergeant Nick Gallagher.

What was happening to her? Why was she allowing this man into her life? She'd sworn so many times not to ever make that mistake again. But somehow, tonight, it felt right for him to be here with her.

## Chapter 6

"Er, let's have some coffee and cookies while the popcorn cools," she quickly suggested.

"Sounds good. All that tree trimming has made me hungry."

Allison moved away from him and went to take down cups and saucers. Nick crossed over and took a chair by Benjamin, who looked up and gave him a mischievous grin.

Allison turned just in time to see Nick stroke a gentle hand across the top of Ben's red hair. The sight made everything go still inside her. There had been so many times in the past when her heart had ached because her son didn't have a father, had ached because there was no one other than herself to hug him tight, make him feel loved and secure. To see Nick with her son did something strange to her heart.

Clearing her throat, she picked up the coffeepot. "We've been so busy with the tree I haven't had a chance to ask you what you think about your brother getting married."

Nick watched her pour the coffee. Her head was bent, her face obscured by her tawny hair. It was like a curtain of silk, one that Nick would like to slip his fingers into. "I'm very happy for him."

She carried the coffee over to the table and placed his directly in front of him. As she leaned over his shoulder, Nick breathed in the flowery scent of her skin.

"So am I," Allison said. "Olivia is so kind and beautiful. I can't imagine anyone better for Sam."

Nick took a sip of coffee, then reached for a cookie. "Yeah. Apparently they'd been carrying a torch for each other all these years. Can you imagine it?"

"I guess time or distance can't keep two people apart if they're truly meant to be together."

Nick studied her quiet face. "You think people are predestined to meet and fall in love?"

*Fall in love.* Just to have him say those words to her made her a little crazy. Her hands trembled slightly as she reached for her coffee. "It happened for Sam and Olivia."

But not for her. He could hear the words in the sound of her voice, even though she hadn't spoken them. "This will probably sound crazy, but I—I'm feeling a little deserted now that Sam has Olivia in his life," he confessed.

"I thought you two didn't get to see each other that much anyway," she said, a little surprised by his admission.

Nick shrugged, feeling foolish now that he'd spoken his feelings out loud. "We don't. But when we were growing up, it was always just me and him. And when I happened to get leave and come home for a visit, I always knew it would still be that way. But it won't anymore."

Since Allison had been deserted most of her life, she could certainly relate to what Nick was feeling. She gave him an encouraging smile over the rim of her coffee cup. "Well, you won't feel that way when you find the woman you want to marry."

Before, if anyone had connected him to the word marriage, he would have found it highly amusing. But he wasn't laughing now. Coming home and finding his brother so happy and eagerly waiting to bind himself to the woman he loved had done something to Nick. Not to mention what Allison was doing to him now.

"Or maybe you already have found her," she added, her eyes dropping to his strong fingers resting against the tabletop.

Nick's brows slowly inched upward. Had he already found that woman? he wondered. Was he looking at her this very moment?

"What do you think?" he asked quietly.

She shrugged, hoping to appear unaffected by his question. "I think it will be a long time before you hear wedding bells."

That's exactly what Nick had been telling himself, too. That he was having too much fun being a carefree bachelor. But now as he looked across the table at this beautiful, sensitive woman, he wanted to assure her that he wasn't really a playboy.

"Well," she said, setting down her mug, "if you've had enough coffee, we should start to work on the popcorn. Ben will be conking out before long."

"Sure," he said compliantly, setting his cup aside. "I'm ready when you are."

Relieved, Allison left the table and went to gather everything they'd need to make the garland. While she did she told herself to pull herself together. There wasn't any excuse for allowing Nicholas Gallagher to shake her so. He was just a soldier home for the holidays. But she was beginning to like him. She couldn't seem to help herself and that scared her terribly.

The two of them decided to do their work sitting on the floor in front of the fireplace, where the house was the warmest. Nick turned on the radio to a station that was playing mostly Christmas songs.

Sometimes he sang along, while Ben helped by handing the two adults popcorn and cranberries to string.

At first Allison wanted to hurry and finish the job. She wanted to put an end to the evening and get Nick out of her house. He was making the whole thing too pleasant for her and Ben. He was making her wish for things that she didn't have—like a real home with a husband who truly loved her. He made her wish that Benjamin could have a father to love him and guide him as he grew. But after a while, she pushed the serious thoughts out of her head and began to enjoy herself. It was Christmas, after all, she told herself. She was entitled to get into the spirit.

The garland was finished and Allison was draping it on the tree when she noticed that Benjamin had fallen asleep on the floor beside Nick. She watched as Nick got up and placed the child on the couch.

"We didn't get to the star and I wanted Benjamin to put it on top of the tree," Nick said as he placed a crocheted afghan over the sleeping child.

Allison looked over her shoulder to see that her son was still sound asleep and Nick had come to stand behind her. The idea that Ben would no longer be an interruption made her feel breathless and wary of Nick. Was he finally going to tell her it was time for him to go home?

"I'll let him do it tomorrow evening before he goes to the baby-sitter." Turning back to the tree, she pretended the garland needed a bit more adjusting.

"You're not letting him come to the wedding?"

Allison shook her head. "If he were a bit older I would. But I can hardly be a bridesmaid and watch him, too. It's no problem, however. Gayle, my girlfriend at work, has offered to keep him for the night. And he adores her. She lets him have all the chocolate kisses and soda pop he wants. I look for holes in his teeth every time he visits her," she added with a good-natured groan.

"That's good," he said, his eyes gliding down where her hair lay like a piece of pale bronze satin. "I mean, that you won't have to worry about Ben tomorrow night. I'm sure the reception will go on a long time and you wouldn't want to leave the celebrating."

She could feel his breath stirring her hair. She closed her eyes and fought at the weakness filling her limbs. "I'd better put Benjamin to bed," she murmured, "he's had a long night."

Nick moved a step closer and lifted a strand of her hair between his fingers. "Ben's fast asleep. Dance with me."

His voice was close to her ear and sent shivers down her spine. She had to draw in a long breath before she could manage to speak a word. "I—I don't dance."

"I don't believe that. Come here and prove it to me."

Before she could protest, he took her by the hand

and drew her into the middle of the floor. As he pulled her into his arms, Allison caught the devilish grin on his lips, the seductive glint in his blue eyes. He was dangerous, she thought. Perhaps more dangerous than Larry had ever been. Larry had only hurt her on the surface, whereas an entanglement with Nick might reach right down to her heart and tear it in two.

"They're playing 'White Christmas'," Nick murmured as he tucked her head against his shoulder. "That's one of my favorites."

They began to move in a slow, lazy circle around the floor. Allison tried her best to hold herself away from him, but it was impossible with him nudging her right back against him.

He felt so hard and strong. She could feel his arms, his chest, his legs all moving against her, making her senses so muddled it was a supreme effort just to think about his words.

"You like soft music?" she asked.

The disbelief in her voice had him chuckling. "And what do you think I like, Allison? You think I like getting down to hard rock?"

She smiled in spite of the tension building inside of her. "It seems to fit you better."

"Hmm," he said, pressing his cheek against the softness of her hair. "Well, I do like the Rolling Stones. There's something sexy about that sort of raw, hard-driving beat. But then—" his hand moved slowly, gently against her back "—there's something very nice about the slow stuff, too. Don't you think?"

Allison closed her eyes. "I wouldn't know. I don't know very much about music or dancing."

No, he supposed she didn't. He doubted she'd had much of a chance to enjoy music or parties or even a Christmas with a loving family. The thought had his arms tightening around her. "I hope you've enjoyed this evening."

Allison felt cocooned in the strength of his embrace and her heart began to thump rapidly even though they were barely moving to the music. "I haven't had an evening this nice in a long time," she said truthfully.

Neither had Nick. He couldn't ever remember feeling the way he did at this moment. Having Allison in his arms after sharing the evening with her made him realize he didn't want things with her to end. He wanted more time with her. In fact, he could see them like this forever. And that was a scary thought for a bachelor.

His mind was so caught up in his thoughts, he didn't realize she was speaking to him until she tugged at his hand. He looked down at her, his eyes faintly glazed. "Oh, sorry, were you saying something?"

"I was telling you that I really should put Benjamin to bed. He might be sleeping in a draft there on the couch."

Actually, Allison figured her son was plenty warm enough, but she had to come up with some kind of excuse to get out of Nick's arms, and Benjamin seemed to be the most logical one.

"Oh, well, let me carry him for you." Reluctantly, he released his tight hold on her and walked over to the couch.

With her son in his arms, Nick headed down the hallway and into the bedroom. Allison followed them.

"Just a moment and I'll switch on the lamp," she told him, moving to the small light at the head of Benjamin's bed.

This was a scene that was becoming all too familiar, she thought as she watched Nick carefully place her son on the mattress. One that she was going to have to put an end to. Nick might be generous and devilishly charming, but he was also a man who would be gone in a matter of days. He'd go back to the military base and be a soldier once again. She and Benjamin would be completely forgotten. Allison couldn't allow herself or her son to become attached to him.

Nick smiled and said in a hushed tone, "He's probably already dreaming of a big shiny tractor."

"That or a giant Christmas tree," Allison agreed.

She began unbuttoning Ben's shirt, but the simple task could not keep her attention off the man standing beside her. "There's a pair of pajamas in the top drawer of the chest. Would you get them for me?"

Nick went after them while she continued to undress Benjamin. When he returned he handed her the pajamas, then said, "Allison, please don't take offense at this question, but what happened to Ben's father?"

She looked up at him and Nick could see her eyes turning to cold, green stones. "Ben doesn't have a father. Or rather, his father left just as soon as he heard I was going to have a baby. Sound familiar?"

Nick was used to seeing hard, angry looks. As a drill sergeant, he dished out plenty of them himself. In return, his reputation for being tough had earned him a few vindictive glares. But he'd never seen such an embittered look as the one he was seeing on Allison's face now.

"No. Running out on pregnant women is not familiar to me at all."

Something flickered in her eyes before she looked away from him. Nick wondered what it was, what she was thinking. Was she comparing him to the man who had run out on her?

"No. I don't suppose you'd ever get yourself involved with a woman who'd be foolish enough to become pregnant."

"And you think you were foolish?" he asked gently.

Allison went back to fastening Ben's pajamas. For

some reason she wanted to give Nick the impression that she was strong and resilient, that being discarded and deserted by others was something she'd gotten over long ago.

"I was foolish to trust with my heart instead of my head. Now I don't trust at all."

She was too young to sound so cynical, he thought. "Not all men are like—"

"Larry. His name was Larry Kingman," she finished for him. "And no, I don't suspect they are all like him. But I wouldn't even bother trying to find one that wasn't. It would be like looking for a needle in a haystack."

Nick looked away from Allison and down at the sleeping child. To know that some man had hurt Allison that way made him want to track the guy down and kill him with his bare hands.

Nick couldn't stop himself from reaching out to her, from curling his fingers over her shoulder. "You know, Allison, Larry what's-his-name is getting his due."

Allison's own hands stilled and slowly her head turned toward him. "What do you mean?" she asked, as her eyes fastened on his strong profile.

"I mean he'll never know the joy of seeing his son grow. He'll miss hearing his laughter, seeing the excitement on his face at Christmas. The man doesn't know what he lost."

Allison grimaced. "I'm sure Larry would tell you he didn't lose a thing."

Reaching down, he took her hand in his. "I happen to think he lost a hell of a lot," he said softly.

Allison was momentarily paralyzed. She couldn't look away from him, nor could she pull her hand from the warmth of his. "You don't really know me, Nick."

The dark blue of his eyes softened as he looked back at her. "Well, we can do something about that."

No. No! She couldn't let him melt her with just a look and the simple touch of his fingers. She was a stronger woman than that.

"Why would *we* want to?"

Without saying a word, Nick tugged her away from the bed and into the dim shadows of the room. Before Allison could guess his intentions, he drew her into his arms, anchoring his hands at her waist.

Mesmerized, Allison gazed up at him. His face was so close, so dangerously and temptingly close. She could see the deep flecks of blue in his eyes, the faint lines bracketing his lips. Lips that were moving closer, and she couldn't seem to do a thing about it.

Nick wasn't prepared for the jolt of lightning he felt when his lips finally settled over Allison's. He'd expected her to taste sweet and soft and warm. What he hadn't expected to taste was passion, to feel it rushing through him like a quick shot of adrenaline.

He didn't know when his mind went blank, or when his hands clutched her even tighter against him.

Allison could feel the room begin to sway, her knees grow weak, forcing her to reach out and hold on to him. She'd never been kissed like this. She'd never felt like this!

"Marry me, Allison. Say you'll marry me and live with me forever," he whispered, once their lips finally parted.

She stared at him, the desire to both slap him and kiss him again warring like two armies inside of her. "You—you're crazy!"

Maybe he was, but he couldn't ignore what they had just shared in each other's arms. He couldn't ignore the feeling inside him, or what his heart was saying to him. How could he make her understand?

"Maybe it seems that way," he began, only to have her interrupt with a sharp hiss.

"Seems like it? You ask me to marry you after we've shared one evening, one kiss?" With a disgusted groan, she shoved herself away from him.

"Allison, I'm not crazy. I'm in love with you."

Her head snapped up, her eyes narrowed. "Don't insult me by using that word. I know what love means to a man like you. I doubt you've ever loved a woman in your life."

"You're right, I haven't. Until now."

Throwing up her hands, she gave a brittle laugh. "Sure. Just like that other guy who told me he loved me. He meant it, too, for as long as it took him to say it."

Frustrated, Nick rubbed both hands over his face. "I'm not like him."

Her eyes studied Nick warily as she began to back out of the room. She seemed afraid he was going to pounce on her, Nick thought with disbelief.

"Allison, I didn't ask you to go to bed with me. I asked you to marry me!" He'd never uttered the words to any woman before. He'd never wanted to.

"I don't even know you!"

Shaking his head, Nick moved toward her. Feeling utterly cornered, Allison stepped back until she bumped into the doorjamb.

"I don't think that's true at all. I think you probably know me better right now than you ever knew Benjamin's father."

The words struck a chord of truth in Allison, causing her face to turn pale. Still, she wouldn't allow herself to admit that anything Nick was saying could be real or sincere.

"Look, Nick, tonight was…it was nice for a while. But this—" she motioned weakly at him "—this isn't fun anymore. I want you to leave."

Stepping forward, he trailed gentle fingertips down her cheek. "I'll go. But this is far from over between us."

She stared at him. "There is nothing between us to be over," she reminded him.

The grin that spread across his lips was smug and purely male. "You're wrong about that, Allison. And I aim to prove it to you."

Before she could protest, he turned away and left the room. A few seconds later, she heard the sound of the front door closing and then the pickup engine firing to life.

It was a long time before she could bring herself to move from where she was standing and go back to Ben's bed. The child had kicked away the cover. Allison drew the comforter up to his chin, then bent down to kiss his cheek.

"Don't worry, darling, I won't let him hurt us. I won't ever let anybody hurt us again."

## Chapter 7

Allison arrived at work the next morning bleary-eyed and exhausted.

"What in the world happened to you?" Gayle asked as the two women took their morning coffee break. "You look terrible."

Sighing, Allison ran a weary hand through her hair. "That's just what I needed to hear, Gayle."

The other woman grimaced at Allison's sarcasm. "I'm serious. Are you ill?"

Allison shook her head, then tossed her nearly full coffee cup into the trash bin. Her stomach was in such a flutter even a drink of coffee sent it into fits. "I didn't get any sleep last night."

"Ooh," Gayle purred, then grinned like a cat. "I'm

so glad to finally learn you're human like the rest of us."

Allison threw up her hands. "It's not what you're thinking. I didn't spend the night with Nick Gallagher."

"Oh, shoot." Gayle groaned with disappointment. "Didn't he ask you?"

Gayle's question brought a burst of dry laughter from Allison. Lord, if Gayle only knew what the man *had* asked her, she'd probably be rolling on the floor, howling with laughter. But Allison couldn't bring herself to tell her. It was simply too ridiculous to repeat.

As it was, Allison wished that Nick had merely asked her to go to bed with him. That would have been something far easier to deal with. But love? Marriage? What did the man think? That she'd grown up in a cabbage patch? That she would believe anything a man told her?

"No. We, uh, had a nice evening and then he went home. I was just too tired to sleep after that. And I guess I had Sam and Olivia's wedding on my mind."

Gayle's expression turned puzzled. "I thought you were looking forward to the wedding?"

"I am," Allison said. But that was before Nick had gone and proposed to her. Damn the man! Now the whole evening was going to be utter torture if she tried to avoid him.

Gayle pulled the last cashew from the pack in her

hand and popped it into her mouth. "Boy, you sure could fool me. You look about as happy as someone headed to the gas chamber."

Ignoring Gayle's comment, Allison glanced at her wristwatch. "It's time for us to get back to work. Do you still plan on picking Ben up at the day-care center after work?"

"Sure do. And don't worry about a thing. I've got a fun evening planned for me and your son."

"Thanks, Gayle. I'll do something for you as soon as I can."

As the two women left the staff lounge, Gayle waved away Allison's thanks. "Forget it. All you have to do for me is enjoy the wedding tonight— and maybe spend a little more time with this Nick Gallagher guy."

Allison shot her a sardonic look. "You don't ask for much, do you?"

Gayle smiled smugly. "Not really."

It was after her lunch hour, and Allison had just waited on a line of customers when she glanced up to see Nick standing at her teller window.

"Hello," he said, grinning at her shocked expression.

"What are you doing here?"

He feigned a hurt look at her less-than-warm greeting. "Why, Miss Lee, what does a person do at a bank?"

Absently, she tapped a pen against a pad of deposit slips. "They usually make a transaction of some sort."

His grin spread into a full-blown smile, which in turn had Allison's heart beating in erratic little jerks. He was wearing a blue denim shirt with a dark blue flowered tie. She knew if she were to lean over the counter and look at the rest of him, he'd have on close-fitting jeans and cowboys boots, too. She had to admit he was rakishly handsome, but good looks didn't make for solid and dependable.

"Right. A bank transaction. Just what I came here to do." He pulled two large bills from his wallet and placed them on the countertop. "I want to put this in a savings account," he told her.

Propping himself lazily against the teller booth, he leaned his head in closer to hers. Allison glanced wildly around her. Was the man crazy? Why was he doing this to her?

"Do you have a savings account with this bank, er, Mr. Gallagher?" she asked in her most business-like voice.

Still smiling, he shook his head. "No. I want to start one."

Just what she'd thought. The man had no business in this bank other than to harass her. After drawing in a long breath, she said, "Very well, Mr. Gallagher. You'll have to go over to that service desk."

She pointed it out to him. "The lady there will give you a couple of forms to fill out."

"Thank you for your help. Miss Lee," he added impishly.

Allison watched him walk across the lobby while wondering what the man was up to now. It didn't make sense for him to be opening a savings account here when he lived hundreds of miles away.

She was counting out a stack of bills to a customer when Nick returned to her teller window. He stood patiently waiting until the elderly lady finished her business and moved away. Then he stepped up to the counter and gave her a sly grin.

Allison bit her lip to keep from groaning aloud. "I'm working. You need to go."

Nick glanced behind him. "I don't see anyone needing your services right at this moment." He leaned over the counter top. "Aren't you going to ask me what I'm doing in town today?"

Allison found it too difficult to look at him. Each time she did, the only thing she could think about was the way he'd kissed her so passionately.

Fixing her eyes on a cup of pencils near the adding machine, she said, "I know why you came to town. To make a bank transaction."

"True. But I've also been out Christmas shopping."

This brought her eyes up to his face. He was still smiling, but this time there was a smug, secretive look about him. "You look happy for a man who's been out spending his money. I thought men didn't like shopping."

He made a face at her. "I love shopping. And going to the mall at Christmas is much more fun than shopping at the PX." He paused long enough to get her attention. "You're going to love what I got you. Both things. But you can only have one today. The other will have to wait until Christmas Day."

"Nick—you—"

Seeing that he'd done a good job of flustering her made him chuckle under his breath. "Why, you do remember my first name, after all. I was beginning to wonder if you'd slept so hard last night you'd forgotten it."

Slept? She wished she could have slept around the clock. Maybe then she would have wakened to find Nick Gallagher was on his way back to Fort Sill.

"I have no intention of seeing you tonight," she said in a low, fierce voice.

"Of course you're going to see me tonight. We're both in my brother's wedding party, remember?"

"I meant seeing you alone!"

"Oh, I intend to see you alone long before tonight. In fact, I'll be waiting for you in the parking lot after you get off work."

"Nick—"

He pushed away from the counter and gave her a

little wave. "Five o'clock. And by the way," he added in a hushed voice, "you look beautiful today."

Hot faced, Allison turned her back to him and took several long, deep breaths. What was she going to do? The man obviously had no intentions of leaving her alone.

Later that afternoon she left her post for a coffee break. On her way to the lounge, one of the file clerks approached her.

"Allison, do you have a moment?" the middle-aged woman asked. "I'd like for you to look at something."

Allison glanced anxiously at the other woman. "Of course, Helen. Have I made a mistake on some of my work?"

The kindly woman quickly waved away Allison's question. "Oh no. Nothing like that, dear." She motioned for Allison to follow her to a row of file cabinets. "It's just that when I saw the names on these documents I thought—well—perhaps you should see them."

Thoroughly puzzled, Allison waited while Helen searched through several manila folders. "I don't understand, Helen. I—"

Allison's words halted abruptly as Helen handed her the papers. Quickly, she scanned the document. It was an application for a savings account.

"As you can see," Helen went on, "the money deposited goes to your son. And in case of his death you've been named beneficiary."

Nick! Nick had started a savings account for her son! She couldn't believe it!

"Allison, I'm not trying to be nosy, but—do you know this person? This—" She took the papers from Allison and glanced at the signature at the bottom of the page. "This Nicholas Gallagher?"

Numb, Allison nodded. "Yes, I do, Helen. He's a—friend."

The other woman smiled with relief. "Oh, well, that's wonderful then. I was afraid it might have been a kook trying to get to you or something. I guess I've watched too many detective shows on TV," she said with a laugh.

In an effort to hide her distress, Allison laughed along with her. "Uh well, thank goodness Nick isn't a kook."

Helen tucked the file back into the cabinet then gave Allison a broad smile. "One thing for sure, he's generous. He must care about your son a great deal. Just think how the account will have grown by the time he goes to college."

Allison murmured an agreement, then quickly excused herself from the filing room. She had to be alone for a few moments. She had to think! To figure out what she was going to do once she saw Nick again.

\* \* \*

Nick saw her the moment she came out of the building. The breeze was tossing her hair about her shoulders, and she clutched a purple raincoat against her as if she were afraid the wind would snatch it away from her.

He drummed his fingers against the steering wheel, then glanced down at the brightly wrapped package on the seat of his car. He'd told Allison she would love it. But actually his confidence wasn't all that great about how she'd receive the gift. He wanted her to like it. He wanted her to like *him*.

Hell, Nick, you want her to do more than like you. You want her to love you! Marry you! So what are you going to do about it? a voice inside him asked.

Allison's steps slowed the moment she spotted Nick's red sports car parked next to her old sedan. The thought of facing him again made her want to turn tail and run. But where could she go in a parking lot?

Nick got out and stood at the rear fender of his car to intercept her. When she drew near he said, "Four fifty-five. You must have quit early to meet me."

"It's Christmas Eve, Nick. The boss let us off thirty minutes early for an office party."

"And the party is already over?"

She grimaced. "My part of it is. I need to get home early so I can get ready for your brother's wedding," she said, knowing perfectly well he didn't need to be reminded.

"Oh, yes," He said, reaching for her hand. "My brother and Olivia's wedding. Don't you wish it was ours?"

"I don't find that amusing, Nick."

"I didn't mean for it to be," he said, drawing her along to the passenger side of his car. "Slide in. I want to give you something."

"No."

He opened the door anyway and motioned for her to get in. "Let's not stand here and argue. Sam has threatened to break my nose and everything else in my body if I'm not ready on time tonight."

Knowing he wouldn't give up until she got into the car, Allison climbed in and shut the door herself. Nick quickly skirted around the hood and climbed in on the driver's side.

"Why aren't you home helping decorate the house?" Allison asked as he settled himself behind the wheel.

"I have been. There are red and white poinsettias all over the house. I've never seen the old place look so pretty."

As Allison glanced quickly around her, she noticed his car was a small one with bucket seats and built low to the ground. Allison felt as if she were practically sitting on Nick's lap. Her pulse was certainly behaving as if she were. She could feel it hammering away at her temples. "Uh, before you say anything else—" she crossed her legs and looked straight ahead "—you've got to come back into the bank on Monday."

"I'll be gone on Monday."

He'd be gone! She glanced at him, surprised at how much the news took her aback. This was already Thursday. Somehow she'd expected him to be here at least until New Year's. *Allison, are you crazy?* a voice screamed back at her. *You want the man to be gone. The sooner the better.*

Maybe she did. But at the moment she was feeling something strangely close to disappointment. It didn't make sense!

"Well, you'll have to do it through the mail, I suppose."

He studied her face, wondering how anyone could have skin that soft looking. It reminded him of sweet cream, delicious and smooth. "Do what?" he asked.

She frowned at him, then recrossed her legs. "You know what. You can't give Benjamin that money."

He folded his arms across his chest. "I don't know why I can't. Besides, that transaction is between me and Ben. It has nothing to do with you."

Her brows lifted. "Oh?"

"That's right."

"You mean that even if you hadn't asked me to marry you, you would have still made the same gesture?"

"No. I would have probably doubled the amount. As it was, I didn't want to give you the wrong impression."

She made a snorting sound. "You did anyway."

He laughed deep in his throat, a sound that had already grown familiar to her. It was a warm, sexy sound. One that melted her right down to her bones.

"Hmm. In that case, I'll send mother in with another deposit. I want to make sure it's a big nest egg by the time Ben reaches college age."

She wanted to scream at him, but she knew it wouldn't do any good. And how did a woman fight a man who wanted to give instead of take? Maybe the taking will come later, she thought. That's it. The taking would come later, when he'd softened her up and she wouldn't be expecting it.

Deciding it would be better to let the matter rest until later, Allison said, "You mentioned that you had something to give me. Is it something to slip to Olivia before the wedding?"

"No." Reaching behind him, he gathered up the box. "This is for you and no one else."

Allison's first instinct was to give a flat, all-out no. But as he handed the beautiful box to her there was something in his face that stopped her. What was that she saw in his eyes? Eagerness? Hopefulness? She wasn't quite sure. She only knew that she couldn't hurt him by rejecting the gift.

"I'm only opening this because it's Christmas-time," she told him.

"I understand," he said, more than relieved that she hadn't thrown the box in his face.

Quickly she tugged at the red ribbon, then gasped audibly when she lifted the lid. It was a dress! An elegant dress made of royal blue velvet.

"Take it out. See if you like it," Nick urged, not quite sure about the look on her face. She'd gone so white he was afraid she might faint at any moment.

Allison slowly lifted the gown out of the tissue paper and saw that it was floor length and cut on straight lines. The neck was round, the long, close-fitting sleeves cuffless. One peek at the back of the neck told her he'd bought her exact size. How had he known?

"It's—it's beautiful. I don't really know what to say."

"You don't have to say anything. Just enjoy wearing it."

Shaking her head, she looked over at him. "Where would I wear something like this? I've never owned anything like it in my life!"

He took one of her hands and rubbed it between his. "You could start by wearing it tonight to the wedding. But if you already have something else picked out, I won't mind."

She continued to look at him, her mind churning.

"Olivia told you to do this, didn't she? She wanted me to have something to wear to the wedding."

His brows puckered to an annoyed line across his forehead. "No. Olivia has no idea I bought you a dress. Would it have made you happier if it had come from her?"

Allison had to admit that it wouldn't. Even though she knew she shouldn't let it, the idea of Nick buying her something so personal touched her deeply. "I—it doesn't matter. I can't accept it from you. It wouldn't be right."

"Too late. You have to take it."

"Why?"

"I bought it on sale and it can't be returned."

Allison sighed. She knew he was lying, just like he knew she was going to keep the dress.

"If I wear this dress you're going to get the wrong idea," she told him as she carefully placed it back into the nest of tissue paper.

He laughed under his breath. "If you wear that dress, Allison, I promise to have all the *right* ideas."

She pushed the lid down on the box with hands that trembled. How could she deal with this? He was too smooth and persuasive, too charming for someone like her to resist. But she knew that she had to resist. Somehow. If she didn't, her life would wind up torn apart.

"I suppose you think I should kiss you and thank you for the dress," she said without looking at him.

"I'm not asking, but if you really want to, both would be nice."

She could hear a smile in his voice and it compelled her to look at him.

"I do thank you. The dress is lovely. And—" she stopped and drew in a long breath "—I will wear it tonight."

He leaned closer and ran the back of his finger down the side of her cheek. "What about the kiss?"

Her eyes instinctively dropped to his lips, and suddenly all she could think about was how the rest of the world had faded away the moment he'd taken her into his arms and kissed her.

"I don't think—"

"You're not supposed to think about kissing," Nick murmured, his face drawing to within inches of hers. "You just do it."

She could feel his warm breath whisper across her lips, feel his fingers tangle in her hair. Every sense she had was swiftly mesmerized by him. She wanted to touch him, feel him against her once again.

She leaned into him and placed her lips on his. His kiss was gentle, but so thorough that it was a long moment before Allison could collect herself enough to open her eyes and pull the latch on the door.

"I'd better be going. Olivia and Kathleen are expecting me to be there to dress with them," she murmured hastily, then scrambled out of the car before he could stop her.

## Chapter 8

When Allison arrived at the Gallagher house, she was still angry with herself. She didn't know why she was so weak and foolish where Nick was concerned. Granted, he was sexy, handsome and charming, but that wasn't any excuse for her behavior. She'd kissed the man just because he'd wanted her to!

And because you'd wanted to, a voice whispered back at her. You might as well face it.

"Allison, come in, honey," Ella said when she answered the knock at the back door. "Olivia and Kathleen have been asking about you. They're already upstairs in Kathleen's room."

"Oh, I hope I'm not late," Allison said as she

stepped into the kitchen, garment bag and suitcase in hand. "Should I go on up now?"

Ella laughed and motioned to her slacks and sweater. "You can see that I'm far from ready. So don't worry, you made it here in plenty of time." She took Allison by the arm and led her toward the formal dining room. "Besides, I wanted you to see the house before all the guests arrive."

Nick was right, Allison thought as the two women walked into the room. She'd never seen the house looking so beautiful. Everything was polished and gleaming, flowers were everywhere and on the serving table was the most beautiful three-tiered wedding cake Allison had ever seen.

"Oh, Ella, this is all so lovely. You've worked so hard."

"We all have," Ella admitted, then motioned for Allison to follow her to another room.

"I don't think you've ever been in the parlor. I hardly ever open it up. But we decided, since it was such a large room, it would be a perfect place for the ceremony. What do you think?"

Allison thought she'd walked into a fairy tale. The high-ceilinged room was long and blessed with a wall of paned windows covered with antique-lace curtains. Through the draped swags, Allison could see the lights of the river traffic twinkling like candles on a mirror.

Centered in front of the curtains was an archway

that was covered with greenery and what seemed like hundreds of white poinsettias. At the base of the arch stood two enormous baskets of red poinsettias.

"Ella, this is absolutely beautiful. Olivia must be so pleased," Allison said as she turned to look at the other end of the room.

In one corner stood a huge blue spruce that had been decorated with meticulous care. The upright piano next to it was draped with greenery and flowers.

Ella motioned toward the folding chairs that had been set up for the guests. "Of course, after the ceremony we'll take these out so there'll be plenty of room to dance."

"Dance? You mean you're going to have dancing, too?"

Ella laughed at her look of surprise. "This is a joyous occasion, Allison, and we Gallaghers like to celebrate."

"We certainly do."

Both women turned at the sound of Nick's voice, and Allison's heart began to pound in earnest. She told herself it was because she dreaded the sight of him, but she knew that wasn't entirely true. Just looking at him turned her knees to mush.

"Hello, Allison. Ready for the wedding?"

His eyes leveled pointedly on hers, telling her he was talking about an entirely different wedding from the one tonight. Her cheeks filled with heat as she looked back at him. "I don't know about me, but I'm sure Sam and Olivia are."

"Well, I'm ready. But," he added with a sly grin, "I don't know about Sam. Maybe I'd better go down to the barn and get him."

Ella snorted and waved her hand at him. "Quit your teasing. Sam's not down at the barn and—" She broke off as the phone began to ring. "I'd better go get that."

The woman left the room in a run. Nick turned to Allison and took the bags from her hand.

"I'll carry this for you and show you where to go upstairs."

"I know where to go upstairs," she said, trying her best to sound frosty.

"Oh," he said, surprised. "I didn't realize you were that familiar with the house."

"I know this house a lot better than I do you," she retorted.

With his free hand, he took her arm and led her out of the room. "Hmm. Well, we'll have to do something about that, won't we?"

She glanced over to see he was smiling at her, his white teeth glinting wickedly.

"Do you ever have a serious thought?"

He continued to hold on to her arm as they crossed the breezeway and headed up the stairs. "When it's required. Why? Would you like me better if I were somber and serious?"

She couldn't imagine him being either of the two. "I would like you better if—if you would quit coming on to me like this."

He laughed and shook his head. "Oh, Allison, I can't believe you're all frost under that red hair. There's got to be some fire there somewhere." He leaned closer and whispered against her ear, "And I'm looking forward to finding it."

Allison was about to jerk her arm loose from the band of his fingers when she realized they had reached Kathleen's bedroom door. He saved her the trouble by releasing his hold on her to rap his knuckles against the wooden panel. "Ladies, it's Nick. I've got Allison with me."

"Don't come in here, Nick! We're not dressed," Kathleen shouted.

"Okay, I'm leaving her on the threshold like an abandoned orphan," he said to the door, then leaned down and gave Allison a quick kiss on the cheek. "See you at the wedding," he whispered.

Allison was watching him bound back down the stairs when Kathleen opened the door.

"There you are," she said, taking a rattled Allison by the hand and drawing her into the room. "Did you see the house? Isn't it beautiful?"

"I—I didn't realize the wedding was going to be this fancy," she admitted. "How many guests are there going to be?"

"We invited fifty. But who knows?" Olivia answered from the connecting bathroom.

"Put your things anywhere you can find a clean spot. Olivia and I have already made a mess in here," Kathleen said as she crossed to a vanity table that was strewn with hairbrushes, makeup and other toiletries.

Allison carried her case over to the bed and laid the garment bag down. She had everything she needed to ready herself for the evening ahead—except for a way to get Nicholas Gallagher out of her hair.

"Allison, I brought three dresses from home that you might want to wear. They're over on the back of that rocking chair."

Allison turned around to see Nick's sister busily arranging her long dark hair. "I, uh… Thanks, Kathleen, but I have a dress with me."

"Oh, let me see," Kathleen said brightly, joining Allison at the bed.

"I hope you think it's appropriate. I haven't been to very many weddings in my life and I've never been a bridesmaid."

Kathleen gave her shoulders an encouraging squeeze. "You'd look beautiful in anything, Allison."

Allison's smile was more than self-conscious as she pulled the dress from the garment bag she'd placed it in.

"Why, Allison! It's perfectly beautiful!"

"Let me see," Olivia said as she came into the room in a long slip and stockinged feet.

"Oh, Allison, you didn't have to buy a dress. And one like this must have cost a fortune!" Olivia scolded as she peered around Allison's shoulder at the blue velvet dress.

"Don't worry about that part of it," Allison said. "I just want to make sure it's the right thing to wear."

"Oh, it's exquisite," Olivia quickly assured her. "But I'm going to reimburse you for it."

"But—"

"There're no buts about it," Olivia interrupted with a wave of her hand.

"Olivia is right," Kathleen added. "This wedding wasn't supposed to put a burden on your pocketbook."

"But it didn't," Allison blurted out.

The two women stared at her and Allison knew her face was turning a bright shade of pink. "I mean, uh…" She might as well tell them, she thought wearily. They'd probably find out anyway. "Nick gave me the dress—as a Christmas gift."

Kathleen and Olivia swiftly exchanged knowing glances, then Kathleen began to laugh.

Allison shook her head so vehemently that her long hair flew around her shoulders. "It's not what you two are thinking. There's nothing like that between us."

"Sure," Kathleen said with a smug grin. "That's

just what Olivia kept telling me during Thanksgiving when she and Sam were having it out. Now she's walking around in a happy fog and about to say her marriage vows."

Grimacing, Allison placed the dress back on the bed. "That's not the way it is with me and Nick. For heaven's sake, I've only known the man three days!"

Kathleen laughed again. "I have a friend who fell in love with her husband the first night she met him. They've been happily married for ten years now."

Olivia, sensing that Allison was uncomfortable with the conversation, gently patted her on the arm. "Don't pay any attention to Kathleen. She thinks she's some sort of matchmaker."

Allison smiled gratefully at the other woman. "Nick is a nice man. But I'm not ready for marriage. Not like you are."

"Well, I'm not going to be ready if I don't get busy," Olivia said jokingly, then reached for Kathleen. "Come on, dear girl, you promised to do my hair."

The two women left Allison alone and she quickly unpacked her things from the suitcase. However, after a moment her attention was pulled back to the dress. She reached over and ran her hand across the incredibly soft fabric. Nick was a nice man, she thought. That much was true. And maybe he did want to marry her. But he wasn't a marrying man. She could see that, even if he couldn't.

The next hour passed in a blur for Allison as the three women hurried to do their hair and makeup, and finally get dressed. Kathleen was the first one ready so she helped Allison with the long zipper at the back of her dress.

"It fits perfectly," Allison said, amazed when she glanced at herself in the mirror.

"Nick has a good eye," Kathleen said with a sly little grin.

"And good taste. You look like a goddess in that dress, Allison," Olivia joined in.

Allison looked down at her bare toes. "I only hope my heels won't be seen under this dress. Navy was the only color I had that would come close to matching."

Kathleen snapped her fingers. "I've got just the thing," she said, hurrying off to the closet.

Allison's gaze followed Nick's sister. How beautiful and exotic she looked in an emerald green dress that swathed her tall, regal figure, she thought.

"I bought these to go with a blue party dress I used to have. They'll be perfect." Kathleen's voice, coming from inside the closet, was muffled. Finally, she reappeared, holding up two royal blue satin pumps with rhinestone clips on the toes. "That is, if they'll fit," she said, handing Allison the shoes.

Allison hurriedly stepped into them. "They're just a fraction loose, but not enough to be a problem."

"I'm glad you two have worked that out because

I need help over here," Olivia cried as she nervously fidgeted with her veil.

Kathleen hurried to help Olivia arrange the filmy net over her blond hair, which had been pulled up into a tight French twist.

Allison stood to one side, thinking she'd never seen anyone look as radiant as Olivia did tonight in white lace and chiffon that billowed out from her tiny waist. Pearl drops hung from her ears, while a strand of pearls encircled her neck.

Yet it wasn't just what she wore or the beauty of her face that made Olivia look so special, Allison realized. The soon-to-be-bride was lit from within, making Allison wonder if that was what real love did to a person. How would it feel to be loved like that? she asked herself. How could any man ever love any woman like that? She'd certainly never experienced it.

A short while later, they heard piano music below, signaling that it was time for them to go downstairs. When it was Allison's turn to enter the parlor and join the rest of the wedding party, she was aware of only two things—that the room was full of people and that Nick, standing proudly beside his brother Sam, had his eyes directly on her.

*Oh, Allison, don't think about Nick. Not now.* But she couldn't stop herself. When Olivia floated down the aisle and placed her hand in Sam's, all Allison could do was think of Nick. And as the minister's soothing voice began to speak, she imagined how it might be if it were she standing in Olivia's place, giving her hand and her heart to Nicholas Gallagher. Would he be a man that would truly love and honor her for the rest of their lives?

"I now pronounce you man and wife. You may kiss the bride," the minister was saying.

Desperately, Allison focused her thoughts back on the ceremony just in time to see Sam lift the veil from Olivia's face and kiss his new wife. While the guests oohed and aahed their approval, Allison found her eyes connecting with Nick's.

She half expected him to give her a cocky wink, but he didn't. The look in his eyes was far from cocky. Instead he looked at her with a longing that stopped her breath in her throat.

Shaken, she jerked her eyes from his and determinedly kept them away, even while she followed the rest of the wedding party back down the aisle and into the dining room.

"The best man is the second man who gets to kiss the bride," Nick said, pulling Olivia from Sam's arm and smacking her warmly on the lips.

S.T., who'd been embracing his newly married son, reached out and grabbed Olivia away from Nick. "Olivia knows which man in the Gallagher family really loves her," he boomed out, and kissed a laughing Olivia on the cheek.

Allison turned away from the sight and blinked at

the moisture stinging her eyes. What was happening to her? She should be bursting with happiness for the couple instead of feeling lost and alone.

"You're crying," Nick whispered next to her ear.

Sniffing, she forced a smile to her face and looked around at him. "Only a little. Anyway, that's what you're supposed to do at weddings. Didn't you know?"

The guests had now filtered into the reception area and were surging around the couple to shower them with congratulations. Nick took her by the arm and guided her to a less crowded part of the room.

"You look positively radiant in that dress."

And he looked all man, she thought, in his military attire. The uniform suited him perfectly and reminded Allison of who this man really was. A sergeant in the army who would soon be rejoining his troops.

His hand slipped to the small of her back, and his touch left her quivering inside, but for some reason she couldn't step away from him.

"Come on, I think it's time we reminded them to break out the champagne."

"I don't drink," she said a few minutes later when Nick returned and offered her a long-stemmed glass.

"Tonight is special. It's Christmas Eve and my brother just got married to one of the prettiest, kindest women in the world. Next to you, that is," he said, then clinked his glass against hers. "You don't have to drink it if you don't want to. But you'll need it for the toasts."

She lifted the glass to her lips and took a guarded sip. After all, a little champagne couldn't possibly be as potent as the man standing beside her, she rationalized.

"You seem awfully happy tonight," she said to him. "I thought you were feeling a little torn about your brother getting married?"

He shook his head. "I felt a little melancholy when I first got home. But I don't feel that way now." He looked over at her and gave her a smile that crinkled his eyes and dimpled his cheek. "Now that I've met you."

Allison was trying to decide what to say to that when S.T. came up to them and slung his arm around Nick's shoulders.

"Excuse me, Allison, but there's someone over here that I want Nick to meet. You can have him back in a few minutes."

Nick started off with his father, but not before he'd winked and said to Allison, "I'll find you."

No doubt he would, she thought. But she couldn't understand why a man like Nicholas Gallagher would want to be with her. More than likely he could have most any woman he set his eye on. So why her? And why was she feeling so flattered when she knew that she was probably nothing more than a holiday fling for the man?

Determined to put Nick out of her thoughts, Allison headed into the crowd. She hadn't yet had a chance to give Olivia and Sam her congratulations. If she was lucky she'd get lost among the milling guests and most of the evening would be over before Nick found her again.

She'd gone only a few steps when Ella snatched her up. "I've been hunting all over for you, honey. I want you to meet Olivia's cousin, John. He drove all the way from New Orleans just to give her away."

"Sure, Ella, just lead the way," she told the older woman, while thinking any man in the crowd would be safer company for her than Nick.

# Chapter 9

An hour later, Allison had given up trying to remember all the names and faces of people she had met. She carried a glass of punch to the parlor and sat on one of the folding chairs that had been pushed against the wall and out of the way of the dancers.

A man Allison didn't know was playing the piano. Each time he stopped, the dancers sent up a howl and he'd start to play again. Allison felt sorry for him, and found it amazing that he seemed to be enjoying himself.

But then, Allison didn't know much about partying or joining in the fun. She knew she didn't belong here. These people were happy and carefree—celebrating came natural to them. She couldn't really remember a time that she'd wanted to dance and sing and laugh. But then she couldn't ever remember a time when she'd been truly, deep-down happy.

"You look like you've lost your best friend. You didn't think I'd forgotten you, did you?"

The voice belonged to Nick, and the sound of it sent her pulse leaping with anticipation. Shifting around on her chair, she saw that Nick had taken the one beside her. His hand reached for hers, and without thinking about it, she curled her fingers around his.

"I was hoping that you had," she told him, even though she knew that wasn't quite the truth.

"You know you don't mean that," he said, bringing his head close to hers. "In fact, right now your eyes are sparkling up at mine."

For the past half hour Allison had told herself she was glad Nick was hung up with the other guests. But now that he was back beside her, holding her hand, she knew that she'd missed him. It was something she might as well face.

"That's just the aftereffects of the champagne," she said, unable to keep a smile from spreading across her face.

"I really doubt those two little sips you had were enough to affect anything about you."

"I don't have much resistance," she said, actually

thinking of him instead of the alcohol. She set her empty punch glass on the vacant seat next to her.

"I'll bet you've been wondering why none of the men have asked you to dance," Nick said.

"I hadn't really thought about it."

From the surprise on her face, he could see that she really hadn't thought about it. How totally guileless, he thought. Didn't she know how utterly appealing she was? Or had the men in her life kicked her around so much that she thought no man would actually want her?

"Half of the men here would like to carry you off to some deep, dark cave and ravish you with love," he teased.

Laughing, she said, "I do believe you do more flattering and exaggerating than anyone I've ever met."

She couldn't begin to know how much he enjoyed hearing her laugh. She did it so rarely. "Well, it's true. But they all know that you belong to me."

"Nick, you're spreading it on a might thick."

He gave her an offended look as he tugged her up from the chair. "I'm not spreading anything on. Mom has already put the word out."

Stunned, Allison stared at him. "What? Are you saying…"

Grinning, he pulled her out among the other dancers, then drew her into his arms. "Mom knows I want to marry you," he said simply.

Allison couldn't believe that he'd taken this thing so far, and it suddenly dawned on her that he was truly serious. He did want to marry her. The whole idea left her so shaken she felt weak.

"You told her?"

His hand came up beneath the fall of her hair to caress her nape. "I couldn't help it. I had to tell somebody."

Unable to meet his gaze, she pressed her cheek against his shoulder. "And what did she think? That her son had gone totally insane?"

Nick's arms tightened around her. "Actually, she thought about it for a minute. Maybe two. And then she said she thought that we were perfect for each other."

"Perfect!" She drew back to look at him. "Nick, the first time I met your mother I believed she was one of the smartest people I know. But now—" She broke off, shaking her head in dismay. "You and I are totally opposite. We'd drive each other crazy after one week!"

His fingers pressed into her neck, urging her face closer to his. "You're driving me crazy right now, Allison," he whispered. "What do you say we get out of here?"

"No! Nick…"

Her warning was ignored. He deftly guided her in and out of the crowd until they were at a door that led onto the front veranda. Rather than make a scene that would surely call attention to them, Allison followed him out into the night. However, the moment he shut the door and the noise of the crowd became muted, she whirled on him.

"Nick, it's cold! And everyone inside saw us come out here!"

Quickly he pulled off his jacket and wrapped it around her. In the semidarkness Allison could see the outline of his broad shoulders beneath the crisp white shirt he was wearing. The fact that he was willing to bear the cold just to be alone with her sent a rush of heat all the way down to her toes.

"I don't care who saw us," he said, his voice thick as he pushed her back against the side of the house. "I want to hold you, kiss you."

His mouth found hers in the darkness. Allison moaned deep in her throat before she surrendered and began to kiss him back. She would hate herself in a little while, she knew. But right now she wanted him so. Just touching him made her senses sing, her body burn.

She lifted her arms and placed her hands on his shoulders. Beneath his thin shirt, she could feel his heated flesh. When his hands clutched her waist and pulled her up against him, she gasped and tightened her hold. She could feel the bridled strength of his body straining to be next to hers and in that moment she knew that she not only wanted his heated passion, she also wanted his love.

"Nick, I—shouldn't be doing this," she breathed, once his lips finally broke away from hers. "You shouldn't be doing this!"

"Allison." He groaned, his hands finding their way to her breasts. "This isn't wrong. I want to love you. I want to worship every inch of you."

The words fired an image in her mind. She slid her hands down the slope of his shoulders and over the rock-hard muscles of his back, and in doing so, unconsciously urged him closer. The scent on his clothes and skin was a little spicy and even more mysterious. It reminded Allison of bare skin and tangled sheets. It also reminded her of the hot yearning that was slowly building inside of her.

"Nick, I can't do that. I can't—"

"Shh. Don't talk. Just put your arms around me and kiss me."

Allison shook her head, but the moment his lips were back on hers she was leaning into him, accepting his tongue as it slipped between her teeth. As he took her mouth completely, his hands slipped to her bottom and urgently lifted her hips up to his.

Instantly, she became aware of his swollen arousal pressing against her, and Allison knew that he was becoming as heated with desire as she was. Another moment, another kiss and she would give him anything, promise him whatever he wanted!

"Nick! Please, I—" She pushed against his shoulders while gulping for breath "—I'm not ready for this."

Nick's mind was so fogged with desire that it took him a few moments to realize that she wanted to end the embrace. When he did, he released his hold on her completely and passed a hand over his face. He was shaking all over, like a man who'd just had his very first taste of passion.

It took several breaths of icy night air and even more moments before his senses cleared enough so he could speak. But before he did, he reached out and gently framed her face with his hands. "Allison, oh Allison," he said, while shaking his head. "I'm not going to take anything you're not ready to give me. Just tell me what you want. What you need from me."

Her hands came up to curl around his wrists. It was frightening how much she wanted this man. Nothing, no one, had ever touched her the way Nicholas Gallagher had. He'd moved with the swiftness of an arrow and that arrow had gone straight to her heart.

"I don't know, Nick," she whispered in a desperate, almost pleading voice. "I guess I want to know that—that when you kiss me, make love to me that you're doing it with your heart. Not just your body." She turned away from him and unconsciously clutched his jacket tightly against her breast.

Nick came up behind her and put his hands on

her shoulders. He could feel her trembling, though whether it was from fear or desire, he didn't know.

"Allison, I've told you I love you. Is it wrong for me to want to show you that love?"

She swallowed as her heart began to thicken with emotions she couldn't begin to understand. "Just because you said you loved me doesn't make it true. Anyone can say those words. Anyone can make promises. But that doesn't mean that a year from now you'll still be around to see them through."

"I will be. All you have to do is give me the chance to prove it."

She wanted so badly to believe him. She wanted so badly for him to love her. But she was too afraid to trust him. Moreover, she was too afraid to trust herself. She'd made a bad choice when she'd given herself to Benjamin's father. How could she ever live through another mistake like that? She couldn't. There just wasn't enough left in her to survive another heartache.

"I can't think about this now," she told him, drawing in a long, steadying breath. "Besides, your brother and sister-in-law are probably opening their gifts. You're going to be missed if we don't get back in there."

It didn't dawn on her that she might be missed, too, he thought. It didn't occur to her that she might be important and wanted by someone. Most importantly by Nick himself. But he would make her see that she was. He didn't know how, but he would.

"Allison? Are you awake in there?"

Groaning, Allison raised up in the bed to see the gray light of morning filtering through the bedroom curtains.

"Yes, Gayle."

"Mommy! Mommy!" Ben cried, racing into the room and throwing himself onto his mother's bed. "Hurry, get up! Santa Claus has come!"

Allison pushed herself to the side of the bed and reached for a heavy robe on a nearby chair. "Really? My goodness, I must have slept right through it. What did he leave?"

Benjamin's eyes were wide as saucers as he tugged on his mother's arm. "A tractor and a fire truck! Come see!"

"I'll be right there, honey," she said, her spirits lifting at the sight of her son's excitement.

After putting on her robe and slippers, she went to join Ben by the Christmas tree. He was so excited he could barely talk as he thrust one toy after another into his mother's lap. One look at the utter joy on her son's face told Allison that all the scrimping and saving she'd went through the past few weeks to get the toys out of layaway had been well worth it.

She was exclaiming over each toy with appropriate oohs and aahs when Gayle called from the kitchen.

"Merry Christmas, Allison! I'm making coffee, I hope you don't mind."

"Merry Christmas to you, and I hope you made a whole potful!"

"Late night, huh?" Gayle asked.

Allison glanced over her shoulder to see her friend entering the room with two cups of steaming coffee. She was dressed in a bright red jumpsuit and a cheery smile lit her gamine features. After only a few hours of fitful sleep, Allison felt dead in comparison.

"Thanks," she told her as she took the coffee from her. "I'm not sure I'm alive yet. Did you have any problems with Benjamin last night?"

Gayle laughed. "Your son is a joy. I hope by next Christmas I'll be pregnant with a child of my own."

"Gayle! You're not even married."

"So? I can hope, can't I? Besides, you're not married and you're making it okay with Ben."

Allison grimaced then took a long sip of coffee before she replied to her friend's observation. "I'm making it, Gayle. But that's all. There's so many things that Benjamin is missing out on because he doesn't have a father."

"I suppose you're right. It's just that I get to wanting a family of my own," the other woman said, then smiled and waved away the serious tone their conversation had taken. "So tell me, how did the wedding go?"

Allison shoved her hair back off her face. "It was beautiful and the house was jammed with people. Sam and Olivia left before nine in order to catch a plane. But the rest of the wedding party and guests remained to eat and dance until midnight."

"Did the newlyweds let anyone know where they were going on their honeymoon?"

Allison smiled wanly. "They went to Telluride, Colorado. Since Olivia has spent the past four years in Africa, she wanted to see the snow and the mountains."

"Mmm, how lovely. I could go for a honeymoon in a mountain ski resort. As far as that goes I'd settle for any kind of honeymoon." A coy smile spread over her face. "So tell me, did you catch the bride's bouquet?"

Allison shook her head. "Kathleen caught it. She's Sam and Nick's widowed sister."

Gayle took a seat on the floor beside Allison. "Maybe a new man is going to come into her life," she said thoughtfully.

Allison's short laugh was full of skepticism. "I don't really think I believe in all those old wedding predictions."

"Well, I don't know the Gallaghers, but I wished I'd been invited to the wedding just so I could have seen this Nick guy you were trying so hard to avoid."

She looked closely at Allison. "Did you two do a little dancing together?"

Oh, they'd done a whole lot more than dancing, Allison thought ruefully. Those minutes she'd spent wrapped in Nick's arms were still so fresh in her mind that the mere memory scorched her cheeks.

"A little."

Gayle frowned at Allison's noncommittal answer. "Just a little? I was hoping all this wedding stuff might have rubbed off on you."

Allison answered by laughing and rising to her feet. "I told Grandmother I'd be there to pick her up by ten this morning. Want to have breakfast with us before we go?"

"Sure. Why not? Maybe while we cook it, I can pry out of you what really went on last night."

Benjamin loved to go to the nursing home for two reasons—he adored Martha, and the old people who resided there always gave him hard candy. This morning as Allison led her son down the long corridor of the building, the two of them were stopped several times by nurses and residents who wanted to wish them a merry Christmas. By the time they reached Martha's door, Benjamin's pockets were stuffed with all sorts of goodies.

"I really want to marry her, Martha. I know that probably seems sudden to you, but—"

Allison, who'd been about to open the door, froze

as she heard Nick's voice coming from inside. What was he doing here? And why was he talking this way to her grandmother?

"Sudden isn't what matters, young man. It's whether you love her or not. That's what counts with me."

Allison still couldn't move, even though she knew it wasn't right to stand outside the door eavesdropping.

"I love her, Martha. I love everything about the woman. She's beautiful and sensitive. Hardworking and determined. She also has spunk, and the way she is with Benjamin—well, I couldn't imagine any woman but her mothering my children."

Tears suddenly stung Allison's eyes and she blinked fiercely in an effort to ward them off. Could he really mean those things? she asked herself. He sounded so earnest and sincere. But then, so had Larry. In the beginning.

"That all sounds good, Nick. But Allison is stubborn, too. She has a mind of her own, if you know what I mean."

Nick chuckled. "Believe me, Martha, I found that out the first night I met her."

"Allison's had a hard time of it. That no-account Clifford never did care about his daughter, or me, as far as that goes. A sister of mine raised Allison most of the time. So my granddaughter really doesn't know what it's like to have a real home. Maybe you're just wanting to marry her because you feel sorry for her? Because you want to give her things she doesn't have?"

Allison wondered what Nick could possibly be thinking now. Could her grandmother be right? Maybe he did feel sorry for her. How humiliating that would be!

Nick let out a snort. "Allison doesn't need pity. I'm the one who needs pity. That woman's tongue is like a double-edged sword. Besides, you and I both know that there're plenty of men out there who'd be more than willing to give Allison a house and security. But I want her to have more than that. I want her to have fun. I want her to have love and passion. She needs more than just a house, and a husband who comes home every night and kisses her on the cheek."

Allison's mouth fell open. He was talking to a ninety-two year old woman about passion? The man was indecent!

She reached for the doorknob again, but still hesitated. Maybe if she waited long enough, her grandmother would put him in his place.

"Now you're talking, son! Give her flowers and perfume and make love to her every night. She needs to remember that she's a woman."

Allison groaned and Benjamin began to tug on her arm.

"Does this mean I have your blessing to marry her?" Nick asked.

This time it was Martha doing the laughing. "I always knew you were going to make a hell of a man, Nicky. I just didn't know how long it was going to take. But I can see you've gotten there and I don't know any other man on earth I'd rather see marry my granddaughter."

But now Allison's thoughts were in such a turmoil it took her a moment to realize Benjamin was pulling at the hem of her coat. She looked down at him.

"Let's go in Mommy. I want to show Granny Lee my new tractor."

Allison knew she could no longer delay opening the door. Drawing in a steadying breath, she twisted the knob and stepped inside.

## Chapter 10

"Hello, Grandmother. Looks like Nick has come to see you."

Martha nodded her coronet of white braids. "We've had a real interesting conversation, too."

Allison tried to keep her expression impassive. "That's good. I told Nick you'd like to see him again." She glanced his way and felt a jolt of connection as their eyes locked. No man had ever looked at her the way Nick was doing. It made her whole body flush with pleasure and unbidden desire.

The old woman peered through thick glasses at her granddaughter and then at Nick. "Well, this time I didn't have any licorice sticks to give you, Nicky."

"I've got a confession to make, Martha. I hate licorice," Nick told her.

The old woman cackled. "Then I know it was my company and not my candy you liked all those years ago." She patted her knee and motioned for Ben to come to her. "Come here, my boy, and let me see what Santa brought you."

As Ben told his great-grandmother all about his new toys, Nick took Allison by the arm and led her out into the hallway. Before she could guess his intentions, he bent his head and kissed her on the lips.

"Merry Christmas, darling."

"Merry Christmas," she murmured. The touch of his lips, the warmth of his voice disturbed her more than she could say, making it hard for her to meet his gaze. When she did finally lift her eyes up to his, she saw that he was smiling and his eyes were dancing with blue lights.

"So what are you doing here this morning? Mom and Dad are expecting you," he said to her.

"I know they're expecting me to bring Ben and Grandmother over for Christmas dinner. So I'm here to pick her up."

Nick frowned thoughtfully. "I thought I told you last night that I would pick up your grandmother this morning and take her to the farm?"

"If you told me that, I don't remember it." But then Allison hardly remembered anything about last night after those reckless minutes she'd spent in Nick's arms on the darkened porch.

"Sorry. I should have called you this morning and made sure of your plans. It would have saved you a trip up here to the nursing home."

Allison shook her head at his apology. "That's all right. Ben was anxious to tell his great-grandmother all about his new toys anyway. Besides, I haven't yet had a chance to tell Grandmother she's going to be spending the day at your parents' house. She might want to go to her own house."

Nick grinned. "I've already told her. She's looking forward to seeing Mom and Dad. You know, they were her friends and neighbors for more years than I can remember."

Allison knew she couldn't argue that point. "Yes, I know. S.T. and Ella still visit Grandmother quite often. But I was just thinking that—"

He frowned. "Thinking what?" he urged.

She shrugged, not knowing how to go on. How could she tell him that she didn't want to spend Christmas Day with him and his family? She couldn't. Not without explaining why. And Allison couldn't do that without giving herself away.

She knew that Nick was aware of just how much he disturbed her, but he didn't know that she was falling in love with him. Allison hadn't realized it herself until a moment ago when she'd walked into her grandmother's room and seen him standing there. And the admission terrified her. She wasn't supposed to love Nick. She couldn't let herself love him!

Her gaze dropped away from his to the tiled floor beneath their feet. "I heard you two talking, earlier."

His mouth twisted in a wry grin. "I know. I could tell the moment you came through the door. You looked like you wanted to kill me."

No, that wasn't what she'd been feeling at all. But better to let him think so, Allison decided. If he had any idea that her heart had softened toward him, he'd waste no time in taking advantage of the fact.

"What were you doing telling her you wanted to marry me? First Ella and now Grandmother! You've gone crazy!"

His laughter drew the attention of a group of people gathered in the hallway several doors away.

"Merry Christmas," he called to them, before turning Allison away from their curious stares. "If this is crazy, it feels wonderful. Come on, let's go get Ben and Martha and go home. Mom's got the turkey roasting and Christmas carols in the CD player. If you want, we can even go to the parlor and do some more dancing."

Allison glanced at his suggestive expression. "I think we've done enough dancing, don't you?" she said hastily, as memories of last night came rushing to mind.

Laughing under his breath, he bent his head and whispered in her ear. "We've only just started, my sweet."

"Ella, you fixed this apple cider just for me, didn't you?" Martha asked.

Everyone had gathered in the den and Ella was passing mugs of warm apple cider to the adults. "I thought you might enjoy it," she said, taking a seat beside the older woman.

Martha took another sip and smiled contentedly. "You sure thought right."

Benjamin was by the Christmas tree, busy tearing into the gift Nick had given him. He pulled away the last bit of wrapping paper to reveal a shiny red wagon. The moment he realized what it was, he squealed at the top of his lungs. Allison watched in dismay. Nick had already started a savings account for Benjamin, one that she still didn't want to accept. Now he'd given him another gift. She didn't know what to think, or what to do about it.

Nick laughed, amazed at how wonderful it made him feel to see such joy on Benjamin's face. He'd never thought of himself as a father before. He'd always believed that was something Sam would be a lot better at than himself. Sam was quiet and patient and responsible, all the things a parent needed to handle a child as it grew into adulthood.

But now that Allison had come into his life, Nick

was beginning to look at himself in all sorts of ways he never had before. And he realized he *wanted* to be a father. Not only to Benjamin, but to children of their own.

"How about a ride?" he suggested to the boy.

Ben quickly climbed into the wagon. "Yeah! Go for a ride!"

Nick glanced over at Allison, who was sitting with Ella and Martha on the couch.

"Maybe Ben should have his coat on," he said to her. "Do you know where it is?"

"I'll get it." Nodding, she left the room to fetch Ben's coat from the kitchen. Yet before she could return to the den, Nick had pulled Ben and the wagon through the house and into the kitchen.

"Put your coat on and join us, Allison," he said with a grin. "Ben might even let you ride behind him."

Allison knew she should probably say no. But she couldn't find it in her to voice the word. It was Christmas and her son was having the time of his life. She wanted to share in his joy, not miss out on it because of her feelings for Nick.

"Okay. But I warn you—I'm very heavy."

Nick laughed. "I've carried weapons on five-mile marches that were heavier than you are."

"Bragging, are we, Sergeant Gallagher?"

"Nick is strong, Mommy. See, he's big and tall."

"So he is," Allison said, her eyes gliding up and

down Nick's long, lean body. This morning he had on blue jeans that hugged his muscular thighs and hips. Plenty of power there, she had to admit.

Her eyes moved upward to the thick sweater patterned in hues of blue and gray. The bulky garment accentuated the width of his shoulders and reminded Allison of how strong Nick was. She could still remember the feel of him when she'd stood locked in his embrace. The scent of his skin, the warmth and strength of his muscles flexing beneath her hands were still vivid in her mind. She didn't think there was anything about Nicholas Gallagher that she would ever be able to forget.

"Don't you think you'd better get a coat, too?" she asked him. "It looks like it might begin to snow."

One of his brows lifted in surprise, not at her weather prediction, but at her subtle concern for his comfort. He reached for the old jacket Sam always left hanging by the kitchen door.

"Would you really care if I caught cold?" he asked as she bundled herself and Benjamin in their coats.

Allison's hands paused in the act of tying Benjamin's hood. "Of course I would care. You wouldn't want to go back and spread all those germs among the troops."

He frowned, but Allison missed it as she continued to fuss with Benjamin's clothing.

So she was already looking ahead to his leaving, he thought. Funny, he wasn't. For the first time in more than six years Nick wasn't ready to leave the farm. And that surprised him. Before, he'd never felt like he truly belonged here. He'd never felt there was any reason for him to stay around. It was one of the reasons he'd joined the military in the first place. Now Allison was making him look at things in a totally different light.

"Your concern for the troops is endearing, Allison, but I'd rather hear it's me that really concerns you."

"Oh, you do," she said, her voice suddenly light and teasing. "I'm concerned that you really might not be able to pull Ben and me in this new wagon."

Liking the playful glint in her eyes, Nick laughed. "Get in and I'll show you," he told her, motioning with his head to the empty spot behind Benjamin.

"I will. When we get outside."

"There's no need to wait. Get in. I'll give you the same ride I used to give Sam and Kathleen."

She gave him a wary look as she seated herself behind her son. "Now, Nick, you can't be reckless with Ben in here."

He laughed again as he picked up the handle of the wagon. "Ben, hold on real tight to your mommy's legs," he told the child, then he called out loudly over his shoulder, "Come shut the door behind us, Mom."

The next thing Allison knew they were flying out the door and across the back porch. When they hit the wooden steps, Benjamin's high-pitched laughter drowned out his mother's squeal of shock. She shut her eyes and hung on for dear life as they thumped and bumped their way to the bottom.

"Nick, let me out of here!" she cried when they landed on the sidewalk.

"Not on your life!" He laughed as he took off in a sprint across the backyard and out the gate.

While Benjamin urged him on with squeals of joy and wild giggling, Allison begged him to stop each time her bottom slapped against the wagon bed.

Finally out of breath, Nick stopped. But by then they had passed the big barn and were out in the fields. Allison quickly clambered to her feet before he could get his second wind. But catching his breath ended up taking more time than she expected—each time he looked at her indignant face, he burst out laughing.

"Okay, okay. You've had your fun, putting me at your mercy," she said. "But I'll never be guilty of trusting you again."

"Oh, honey." He groaned. "You know that was fun." Drawing her into the circle of his arms, he brushed the tangled hair out of her eyes. "Just ask Ben. He's ready to go again."

"He might be, but I'm not," she said, rubbing her bottom with both hands. Suddenly the image of how silly she must have looked bouncing in the wagon had her laughing. "I really wish I could pull you, Nick. I'd give you the ride of your life."

"I don't doubt that," he said, thinking she'd already started him on a ride that he'd never expected to take. But now that he was on it, he didn't want to stop. Nor did he want to turn back.

"Come on," he told her, "you can walk with me, while I pull Ben."

They started back in the direction of the barn. As they walked slowly along, Nick reached for her hand and Allison gave it to him.

Halfway there snow began to fall. The flakes were fat and wet. By the time they reached the barn, it had covered their clothes and hair.

"I don't think I've ever seen a white Christmas," Allison said, her eyes glowing with pleasure as the three of them watched the falling snow from inside the barn.

Nick looked down at her and smiled. "That's why I ordered it just for you."

She lifted her eyes to his and felt her heart turn over at the tender look on his face. "I didn't know Mother Nature had to follow a drill sergeant's orders."

The sculptured curve of his mouth moved into a smile. "We have more clout than you know."

She smiled back at him. "So I see," she said, then turned back to watch the snow. "Did you—were you sent to the Persian Gulf while Desert Storm was going on?"

Nick wondered what had prompted the question.

Was she thinking that she didn't want to involve herself with a man who might someday have to face the dangers of combat?

"No, I wasn't. Although I will admit at the time I was hoping like hell I'd get my orders to go."

Her head jerked around. "Why? Why would you want to put your life on the line? Do you enjoy living on the edge that much?"

Nick shook his head. "No. It's not that." He pressed both of her hands between his. "Many of the troops I had helped train went over there to fight. I wanted to be with them. You see, when you've spent weeks and weeks with a group of young men you begin to think of them as your family. Throughout their training they looked to me for guidance, to get them through things they'd never faced before. I feel sort of like a father to them, you know. And a father wants to be around when his children are faced with danger." His shoulders lifted and fell. "But my job is to train, so I was kept here in the States."

She studied him with thoughtful eyes. "You're a young man. I can't imagine you shouldering such a responsibility."

His expression twisted ruefully. "Yeah, well, you're not the only one who thinks I'm irresponsible."

Allison suddenly felt as wounded as he looked. She hadn't meant to hurt him. In fact, hurting him in any way was something she couldn't bear to think about.

"That's not what I meant, Nick."

"It doesn't matter. I'm used to it," he said curtly.

Reaching for the handle of the wagon, he pulled Ben over to an area of the barn where Sam stored several pieces of farm equipment.

Allison strolled along beside him. "What do you mean?" she asked, surprised at how much she wanted to know more about this man.

Nick laughed, although Allison caught a hint of sadness in the sound.

"From the time I was big enough to follow after Sam, I was always in some kind of trouble. And at times, I even got him into trouble."

"I can't imagine that," she teased, hoping to see him smile again. Until now, she hadn't realized how much she liked seeing his impish grin, the sheer joy of living written on his face.

"Well, imagine it. I couldn't plow worth a damn. Didn't want to, in fact. I'd start daydreaming and end up getting the rows as crooked as a snake. Or I'd slip off to the river or over to your grandmother's instead of doing whatever job my dad had given me to do."

"That's kid stuff."

"But I didn't change, Allison. Even when I graduated high school I was still raising hell. I didn't want to be a farmer. I couldn't be—not like Sam."

"You're not like Sam," she reasoned.

"No, I'm not like Sam. But I always wanted to be."

They stopped beside an old red tractor. Nick lifted Benjamin out of the wagon and sat him in the driver's seat. The boy immediately grabbed the steering wheel and began making the noises of a motor as he pretended to drive.

"Did your father want you to be a farmer?"

Nick's brows pulled into a straight, grim line. "At first he did. But when he saw I couldn't cut it, he wanted me to go to college, make myself into something important." Nick shook his head at the memory. "We argued for several months about it. I couldn't see myself as a doctor or a lawyer, jobs that would confine me inside four walls. Besides, I thought he only wanted to send me off to college to get me out of his hair."

Allison shook her head at his misguided thinking. But then she knew how mixed-up a person could become when feeling unloved and unwanted. "So how did you end up in the army?"

He let out a wry laugh. "I just happened to be going by the recruiting station one day and on impulse I stopped and went in. I signed up without a second thought."

She let out a breath, thinking she definitely hadn't been wrong in calling this man impulsive. "And have you regretted it?"

He looked at her, and suddenly a slow smile began

to spread across his face. "No. Not ever. It was the best thing I've ever done in my life."

"I'm glad," she said, and meant it.

For some reason, knowing this man was happy made her feel happy. Which was ridiculous. She'd only known him a few days and his life was his own business and nothing to do with hers. Still, she felt happy at the moment and she crooked her arm through his with an ease that would have shocked her two days ago.

"Why don't we go look at the hogs? S.T. tells me he has a champion sow."

Laughing, Nick reached to lift Ben from his perch on the tractor. "He does and she's almost as pretty as you."

"Oh, thanks." Allison laughed.

## Chapter 11

Dinner was the most enjoyable meal Allison could remember having. Everyone talked and laughed and stuffed themselves on turkey and all the trimmings, not to mention all the pies and candy that Ella and Kathleen had baked last week before the wedding.

After dinner when everyone was lounging lazily in the den, Benjamin was determined to get his Granny Lee into his new red wagon.

"Son," Martha told him with a spritely laugh, "your granny can't fit into that wagon."

Ben looked at his great-grandmother, then back to his wagon. "You'd fit, Granny. Mommy did."

"How are you going to get out of this one, Martha?" asked Ella, who was sitting next to Martha on the couch.

Martha Lee drew her great-grandson close to her knee. "Ben, I wish more than anything that my legs would fit into your new wagon, but your granny is too old. But I'll bet Ella would fit. Why don't you ask her?"

Laughing, Ella warned, "Martha! Don't you do this to me!"

Obviously enjoying herself, Martha urged her grandson over to Ella. "Go ahead," she told him. "Ella won't bite. And maybe Nick will pull you both."

"If Mom can fit into that wagon after the dinner she ate," Nick spoke up teasingly, "I'll pull her and Ben all the way to the county road!"

Never one to back down from a challenge, Ella left the couch and scrunched herself into the wagon, then invited Ben to sit between her legs.

"The parlor and back will be far enough," Ella told Nick as the three of them started out of the room.

Ecstatic at having so much attention showered on him, Ben laughed and squealed with joy while Martha clapped with approval.

Allison took a seat beside her grandmother and reached for her hand. "Are you enjoying today, Grandmother?"

Martha patted the back of Allison's hand. "I'm having a lovely time, dear. I always wanted to have a family like the Gallaghers. But since I didn't, being here for Christmas is the next best thing."

Allison's smile was melancholy as she thought about how she'd always wanted to belong to a family like this one, too. But like her grandmother, Allison was going to have to settle herself for belonging just for today.

Later that evening Allison helped Kathleen and Ella clean the kitchen. By the time they'd finished the task, Martha was growing tired and ready to return to the nursing home. Kathleen quickly insisted that Allison leave Ben with her and her parents while she and Nick drove Martha back into the city.

Snow had continued to fall throughout the afternoon and was beginning to grow deep on the streets, but thankfully Nick's car had front wheel drive and they traveled the distance to the nursing home without incident.

"Let's drive downtown and look at the Christmas lights," Nick suggested.

They had already told Martha goodbye and were now getting back into the car to leave. Allison looked over at him as if he'd lost his senses. "Nick, if you haven't noticed yet, there's several inches of snow on the ground. We need to get home before we get stranded."

He gave her an arrogant grin as he started the engine. "I know there's snow out there. Remember,

I'm the one who ordered it for you. And it's beautiful, isn't it?"

Just as she expected, he turned the car toward downtown Fort Smith. Allison let out an impatient breath. "You are the most reckless, unreasonable—"

"You really mean sweet and romantic, don't you?"

Romantic. The word was enough to set her pulse jangling. All day long Nick's family, Martha and Ben had prevented the two of them from being alone. But now it was just the two of them. Music was playing softly on the radio, twilight was falling along with the snowflakes and she wanted to kiss him so badly that she ached. But she couldn't let it happen.

Running a nervous hand over her tumbled red hair, she said, "No. I meant the first two."

He frowned. "Now don't start getting cold on me just because we're alone."

How could he read her so well? He couldn't know her, she silently argued with herself. He hadn't had time to. But he seemed to just the same.

"I'm not. I'm being sensible."

He smiled, and keeping his eyes on the road, lifted her hand to his lips. "My sensible little Allison. We're perfect for each other."

Goose bumps danced along her arm and shivered down her spine. "What makes you think such a thing?"

He lowered her hand to the console between the seats, but didn't release his hold. Allison looked out the window and told herself it wasn't wrong to enjoy touching him. She was human, after all.

"With your practicality and my—uh, sense of adventure, we can't go wrong. I won't let you become boring and stuffy, and you won't let me grow too reckless or impulsive."

"Where do you get these ideas? I'm beginning to think you've been watching daytime talk shows instead of training soldiers."

Laughing, he glanced at her. "Oh, Allison, this is the best Christmas I've ever had."

His fingers slid between hers and squeezed. Allison glanced at his profile, which was now illuminated by the lights of the dashboard. His face was becoming more than just handsome to her. It was becoming dear and familiar. When she looked into the days ahead, she couldn't imagine what it would be like not seeing him, hearing his laughter or feeling the touch of his hand.

An aching thickness filled her throat, forcing her to swallow before she could speak. "Of course it's been a good Christmas for you. Your brother got married."

"Yeah. Brother Sam got married," he said fondly. "But that's not the reason. You've made this Christmas special for me, Allison. I hope I have for you and Ben," he added.

"You have," she quietly admitted.

"Then why is there such a sad look on your face?"

She was going to have to tell him goodbye. Not just for days or months, but goodbye forever. And to think of it was twisting her apart.

Shrugging one shoulder, she turned her head away from him and pretended an interest in the city streets. "I guess I'm just a little sorry to see Christmas go. It has been special this year."

At the next block Nick turned into a parting lot and stopped beneath a street lamp.

"What are we doing?" Allison asked. "This place is deserted."

He switched off the headlights, but left the motor running so the car would stay warm. "That's why I chose it. We've had enough company today."

"Nick, I—"

He shifted around in the seat so that he was facing her. "Before you start putting up a fuss, I want to give you your other gift."

Bemused, Allison stared at the square box he retrieved from the back seat. "Another gift? Nick, the dress was far too much. And I—I didn't get you anything."

Shaking his head, he reached out and touched her cheek. "You couldn't have bought me anything that I would have liked more than what you've already given me."

Her heart was pounding so hard she could scarcely breathe. "What is that?"

"Your company," he answered.

Allison's eyes slipped away from his. He wasn't being trite, she realized. He really meant it. How had she let herself get into this? she wondered. Why had she allowed herself to get close to him? Why did she care about what he said or how he felt?

"Here, I told you yesterday at the bank that you'd like this gift even better," he said, handing her the brightly wrapped box. "So open it and let me see."

"I have the awful feeling that this is something expensive," she said, her fingers toying nervously at the red ribbon. "If it is I—"

Nick couldn't find it in himself to be impatient with her. He knew she'd always had to worry about the cost of things, to be frugal with every penny she earned. It was obvious that she considered money spent on her as wasted. And that tore at him.

"Allison, don't worry. It really didn't hurt my pocketbook. Besides, cost means nothing when I— well, open it."

She did. And for a moment she was certain her heart had stopped beating. It was a ring. Why hadn't she expected it? She should have known what it would be with all his talk of marriage. Yet she'd kept telling herself that talk was all it really was. But now a ring was staring her in the face. A beautiful square-cut emerald encircled with diamonds.

"Aren't you going to say something?"

She was suddenly aware that she'd been staring at the ring for several moments and hadn't yet made a response. Her eyes were shadowed as she looked up at him. "If this means what I think it does, I—I can't accept it, Nick."

Her words knocked the wind out of him—he didn't know why. He should have expected it. All along she'd been swearing that she wouldn't marry him. Why had he thought she might think differently just because he bought her a ring?

"What are you really saying, Allison? You can't marry me, or you don't want to marry me?"

Was that pain on his face? She couldn't bear it if it was, because she was already hurting enough for both of them. "What does it matter?" she whispered.

His hand closed around her chin and lifted her face to the light. Allison prayed that he wouldn't see the moisture in her eyes.

"Just tell me one thing, Allison. Do you love me?"

Unable to face him or the fear rushing through her, she closed her eyes. "Nick, please don't make me…"

Nick groaned with frustration as her words trailed off. "I think you do love me," he said, his voice low and urgent. "You're just afraid to admit it."

Her eyes flew open and she stared angrily back at him. "Why wouldn't I be afraid? Don't I have reason to be?"

He tugged her toward him, and Allison willingly went into his embrace.

"I know, darling," he murmured against her hair.

"I know that you've been hurt. But why are you afraid of me? I only want to love you."

It would be so easy to give in to him, she thought, her cheek pressed against the warm curve of his throat. But what would happen a few weeks from now, or even a few months from now if he realized his impulsiveness had landed him with a wife and child he didn't want? She'd be shoved out; just like before. Just like always.

"I know, Nick. And I love you."

Nick hadn't been expecting the words and it took him a moment to realize she'd actually said them.

"Oh, Allison," he breathed, "do you know how I've been aching to hear you say that?"

She pulled back from him and was stunned to see the unbelievable joy on his face.

"Nick, you're not listening. I—"

"You love me! What more is there to say? We're going to get married tomorrow!" He suddenly frowned and shook his head. "No, tomorrow is Saturday. We'll have to wait until Monday. I'll call my commanding officer and—"

"Nick! I'm not going to marry you." She handed the ring back to him without even taking it out of its velvet box.

He couldn't have looked more stunned if she had slapped him. "Allison, you're the one being crazy now. If you love me there's no reason you can't marry me! Unless—" he paused to study her face "—you don't want to have to uproot from here and follow me to Fort Sill?" His expression suddenly softened and he reached out and threaded his fingers through her hair. "Oh, honey, I know that your job and your grandmother are here, but we'll come back as often as I can get leave. Besides, I've decided that I'd like to put in for a transfer so that I can be closer to my family. Fort Chaffee is less than five miles away from here and—"

"Nick—"

"I know that with all the changes in defense spending we're in a transitional period right now, but if I could get some sort of position there, we could live right here at home."

The ache in her breast was beginning to burn and spread to her throat, clogging it with unshed tears. "It's not any of those things," she said hoarsely. "I can't marry you because I—I know it would be a mistake. You're not ready to get married."

His features suddenly twisted with angry frustration. "How do you know that?"

"Because I can see! I'm not blind! From what your family has told me you've always backed away from the word *marriage*."

He muttered an oath beneath his breath. "That's because I hadn't met a woman I wanted to marry. I hadn't met you!"

Allison shook her head. "No. You came home and you saw your brother getting married and you de-

cided you wanted to be like him—get married, too."
She looked at him, her expression defying him to tell
her she was wrong. "You admitted to me that you
always wanted to be like your brother."

"I won't deny that. I've always looked up to Sam.
I've always wanted to have his solid dependability,
his strength. But that doesn't mean I want to run out
and marry the first woman I can grab hold of just
because Sam has gotten married! It's insane for you
to even think that."

"Is it?"

"Yes! You're trying to find fault with me, when
it's you who can't face reality. You're too afraid to
say you'll marry me. You have it in your head that
I'm going to be just like Benjamin's father. I'm not
him, Allison. Why can't you see that?"

"Well, if I'm that paranoid, you shouldn't want to
marry me anyway," she shot back at him.

He raked both hands through his short hair.
"Damn it, Allison, I love you. Why are you being
so stubborn?"

Tears swam in her eyes, then brimmed over onto
her cheeks. "You don't know what it's like to have
your heart stepped on like it—" her voice caught in
her throat "—like it was some useless old rag. But
I have, Nick. And it turns me cold with fear just to
think of putting myself in that kind of vulnerable
situation again."

He threw up his hands. "So what do you intend

to do? I'd like to know. Are you going to simply tell yourself to forget that you love me?"

When she didn't answer he took her by the shoulders, forcing her to look at him. "We could have a wonderful life together, Allison. Are you going to deny us that life because you're afraid I'll turn out to be a bastard like your father was, or like Ben's father was?"

She was quaking like a leaf. Not from pain or fear, but because she wanted this man so badly. It was all she could do to keep from throwing herself against him, promising him anything just to feel his arms around her. And that kind of wanting *was* insanity, she thought numbly.

"I have a son to consider, Nick. I want what's best for him."

His blue eyes searched her face. "Do you? I'm beginning to wonder."

She frowned. "What does that mean?"

His hands lifted from her shoulders to gently frame her face. "Have you thought that you might be denying Ben the father he needs, just because you're too afraid to let yourself live again?"

"It's not living I'm afraid of, Nick. It's you! You're not the kind of man I need in my life."

His jaw grew rigid with anger. "What the hell do you want, Allison? Would I be more acceptable if I went out and bought myself a pair of eyeglasses and a pipe, if I promised to sit in an easy chair every night and read the paper just so you'd know I was being a quiet, practical man?"

Dropping his hands from her face, he quickly slid back behind the steering wheel. "Thanks, but no thanks, Allison. Life's too damn short to be wasted. If that's what you want, then you're looking at the wrong man!"

Before Allison could say anything, he jerked the gearshift into reverse and backed onto the street. It was just as well, she thought sickly. There was nothing she could say now that would make either of them feel any better.

"Here," he said, carelessly tossing the ring box into her lap. "You can keep it. Just tell everybody some fool bought you a fashion ring for Christmas."

Allison was thankful that darkness had come to hide her tears. At least Nick would never know how much giving him up had hurt her.

Clutching the box in a fierce grip, she stared numbly out the window at the falling snow.

## Chapter 12

Allison hadn't known a house could be so quiet until she'd put Benjamin to bed later that night. Up until then, his laughter and chattering had helped to distract her thoughts from Nick. But now they were pushing at her from all directions, and along with them came an unbearable sadness.

With a sigh of resignation, she turned away from her sleeping son and moved over to the narrow window a few steps away. The snow had finally stopped falling. She supposed Nick had ordered it to, she mused. Just like he'd tried to order her to marry him.

*We don't know anything about wishes in the army, Allison. We only know about orders.* Her mouth twisted as his words ran through her mind. She could well believe that now.

Determined to shake her dismal mood, she left the bedroom. She couldn't dwell on Nick anymore, she firmly told herself. She'd done the right thing. Marrying him would have been a foolhardy, impulsive, dangerous thing to do. It was all for the best that she'd finally made him see it, too.

Yet as soon as she stepped into the living room and saw the blue spruce with its twinkling lights and homemade decorations, she wanted to burst into tears. She'd laughed more that night than she could ever remember, and when Nick had danced her around the room she'd felt like she was dancing on the clouds of heaven.

Desperate now, she went to the kitchen and decided to brew herself a cup of tea. She might even turn on the TV. Maybe there would be a Christmas special airing that would hold her attention.

The telephone rang as she was pouring hot water into the teapot. She dropped in the tea bag and hurried to answer it.

"Hello."

"Allison, this is Kathleen. I was just calling to see if you were all right."

Puzzled by Kathleen's suggestion, Allison eased down onto the edge of the couch. "Yes, I'm fine. Why shouldn't I be?"

There was a pregnant pause before Kathleen said,

"Well, to be honest, things seemed pretty strained when you and Nick came back from town. And the way you grabbed Ben and rushed home, I couldn't help but think something had happened between you two."

Allison let out a heavy sigh. She knew Kathleen was truly concerned, but talking about Nick right now was just too painful. "Look, Kathleen, I appreciate your kindness, but I—I don't want to talk about it."

There was another pause, during which Allison closed her eyes and gripped the receiver.

"Then something did happen between you two," Kathleen went on.

"It doesn't matter, Kathleen. It all ended before it ever got started. So there's nothing to worry about."

She was doing her best to sound cheerful, but didn't seem to be convincing Kathleen. Allison was sure that Nick's sister had some kind of sixth sense where people and their feelings were concerned.

"I am worried, Allison," she said, lowering her voice to an urgent whisper. "I'm worried about my brother. He's in a hell of a mood over here."

Obviously someone had come into the room where Kathleen was using the phone. Was it Nick? she wondered. "What—what do you mean?"

"Oh, he's pretending everything is all right," Kathleen continued quietly. "But I can tell it isn't.

He's already been on the phone twice, trying to get his commanding officer."

Allison sat up straighter. "Why?"

"I don't know. He wouldn't tell me. In fact, he bit my head off when I asked." She stopped, then let out a heavy sigh. "Allison, I'm not trying to pry or matchmake or anything like that. I love you and Nick. And you don't have to tell me anything if you don't want to. But if I could lend a hand…"

She trailed off helplessly while Allison rubbed her forehead wearily.

"Kathleen, Nick asked me to marry him. And I had to turn him down. I—I couldn't—" Tears were suddenly clogging her throat, preventing her from saying any more.

"Oh Allison, why—"

"Goodbye, Kathleen," she said on a choking sob and quickly hung up the phone.

Allison slept so fitfully that night that she woke up feeling even worse than she had when she'd gone to bed. However, Benjamin woke in a cheerful mood, talking more than usual between bites of oatmeal.

"When's Nick coming, Mommy?"

A pain lanced through Allison's breast as she looked across the breakfast table at her son. "Nick won't be coming today."

"Why won't he?"

Allison thoughtfully placed her coffee cup back on its saucer before she answered him. "Because— well, because Nick has to get ready to go back to his home."

"Where is that?" Ben asked, cramming another spoonful of oats into his mouth.

"A long way from here," she said carefully.

Benjamin was old enough to understand what far away meant and he looked at his mother with wide, worried eyes. "Won't he come back?"

"He'll come back, sometime," she told him. But not to us, she thought. He'll never come back to us.

Benjamin began to cry—something he rarely did—and the sight of tears rolling down his cheeks tore a hole in her heart. But what could she do about it? She couldn't promise him things that could never be.

Quickly, Allison left her chair and went around the table to her son. "Honey, don't cry," she told him, drawing him into the comforting circle of her arms. "You'll get to see Nick again. But right now what do you say we get dressed and go see Granny Lee?"

"Okay," he mumbled, scrubbing at his eyes with the backs of his hands. "But I still want Nick to come."

Allison passed a hand over his hair. "I know," she said gently. "You like Nick, don't you?"

He nodded and Allison felt the hole in her heart tear a little wider. "Yes, I know. So do I."

\* \* \*

When Allison and Ben entered the nursing home a little later that morning, Martha was sitting in the lounge with some of the other residents. Allison made a point of visiting with the whole group for a few minutes before asking her grandmother if she'd like to walk to the sun room, which was on the other side of the building.

"I'm always ready to walk," the old lady told her while reaching for her cane. "Keeps a body young, you know."

As they started down the wide corridor, Allison matched her steps to her grandmother's slower pace and held on to Benjamin's hand to make sure he did the same. "Well, I really wanted to get you away from the crowd so I could talk to you."

Martha Lee glanced over at her granddaughter. "Figured that."

"It's about Nick," she began, knowing there was no use beating around the issue with her grandmother. Martha was too old and too wise to have any tolerance for evasiveness.

"Figured that, too," she said.

"I don't know how to start," Allison said with a groan.

Martha's hand came up and waved through the air with a choppy, impatient motion. "Honey girl, I know the man wants to marry you. Just tell me what you said. Start there."

"I told him I couldn't marry him."

Just saying the words made Allison's throat ache with tears and she hated herself for being so weak and vulnerable.

"Well, then, guess that's that, isn't it?" Martha said.

Allison looked at her grandmother. She'd been expecting to hear more than that. "Is that all you have to say?"

"What do you want me to say? Sounds like you've already figured it out in your mind and given him your answer."

Allison's shoulders sagged. All that was true. She'd thought it over. And over. And she'd told Nick she couldn't marry him. There wasn't anything else to do about it, she supposed.

"I guess I just wanted to hear you say I'd done the right thing," Allison mumbled.

By now the three of them had reached the solarium. Martha took a seat on a couch flanked by two tall fig trees. Allison sat beside her, while Benjamin chose to sit on the floor and push the small police car he'd carried with him.

Martha drew Allison's hand onto her lap and patted it with her thin, frail one. "The way I see it, you don't need me to tell you anything if you're sure about your answer."

Grimacing, Allison shook her head. "I was sure about it. But I…" She squeezed her grandmother's hand. "Oh, Grandmother, I've never felt so miserable in my life."

"Because you love him."

Allison nodded glumly. "Yes, I do. But I know a marriage between us would never work. He's—he's nothing like I am."

Martha frowned. "How do you know that? You don't know what kind of woman you'd be if you had a man that really loved you."

And did she think Nick would really love her? Allison wondered. It sounded that way. "Grandmother, Nick isn't like other men."

"No. And thank God for that," she said tartly.

Allison arched a brow at the old woman. "Why do you say that?"

Martha made another impatient gesture. "You deserve a man who will give you a life, not one who will turn it into drudgery like that fool son of mine did to your poor mother."

Allison looked sadly at her grandmother's wrinkled but still beautiful face. "My father hurt you terribly. I don't know how you could still call him your son."

"Ain't no use denying the facts, child. I gave birth to Clifford. And when he started to go bad, it did hurt. It hurt because I blamed myself and your grandfather, God rest his soul. But after a while I realized some people just have an evilness in them that never comes out. That's the way with Clifford. He'll be evil till the day he dies. That's why you shouldn't dwell on him, or that young boy in college who hurt you. All that is gone and in the past, Allison. Neither one of them is worth a second thought. So don't give 'em one."

Tears brimmed in Allison's eyes. Martha fished a tissue out of her sweater and handed it to her. After she had wiped her eyes, Allison said, "Nick is a good man, Grandmother. But he scares me."

Martha laughed. "I reckon any man like him would be a little scary. But you're a brave woman, aren't you?"

Allison dabbed at her bleary eyes. "I want to be."

Martha was silent for a moment, then, with a wan smile, she said, "Something tells me, child, that if you put your hand in Nick's and said 'I do,' you wouldn't be afraid at all."

Allison looked past the wall of plate glass to the cloudy sky beyond. "He gave me a ring, Grandmother. An emerald with diamonds all around it. I never thought any man would buy me a ring like that. Especially not a man like Nick."

Martha tapped her fingers against the arm of the couch and smiled to herself. "Guess you gave it back to him?"

Not looking at her grandmother, Allison shook her head. "He wouldn't take it back. He—he was too angry. I think he'd be perfectly happy if he never saw me again."

Martha's lips pursed thoughtfully as she studied her granddaughter's profile. "Well, child, like it or not you'll have to see him again."

Allison whirled back around to the old woman. "Why?"

Lifting her frail hand, the old woman said, "To give him back the ring. It just wouldn't be respectable for you to keep it."

Allison shook her head with weary frustration. "I'll give it to Ella. She'll see that he gets it back. Otherwise, if I try to give it to him…well, Nick is so—unpredictable he might just throw it in the hog pen."

Martha snorted. "Hmm, well, we wouldn't want that now, would we?"

There was a faint smugness to Martha's voice. Annoyed by it, Allison arched a brow at the old woman.

"Grandmother, you're supposed to be advising me, not patronizing me."

Martha clicked her tongue. "I wasn't patronizing you. I was just thinking."

"About what?"

"About how it would feel to be young and in love." A wan smile crossed her face, as though she were remembering and the memories were fond ones. "And I'm wondering, too," Martha went on, "if you might have turned Nick down because of me."

Surprised, Allison said, "Of course not. Why would you think that?"

Martha studied her granddaughter for a long moment. "Because I'm old and I'm the only relative you have. You might not want to move away because you'd feel guilty about leaving me behind. You know, Allison, that I'd be angry if that was the way of it."

It probably wouldn't surprise Martha to know that Nick was sensitive to Allison's feelings where her grandmother was concerned. Martha seemed to already know the kind of man Nick had grown into, just from the boy she used to know.

"I wouldn't want to leave you," Allison confessed.

Martha smiled and patted her knee. "I have lots of friends here, Allison, and I'm well cared for. I got to live for many years with the man I loved. It would make me happy for you to have the same thing."

Yes, but was that man Nick? Allison wondered. She supposed her grandmother couldn't tell her that. Nothing could, except her own heart.

"Where the hell is he?" Nick barked into the telephone. "This is the fourth time I've called and you still can't locate him! What imbecile left you in charge of his office anyway? I want—" Nick's face grew dark and thunderous as the caller interrupted him with another useless string of excuses. "Yes, I know it's Christmas, but—oh hell, forget the whole damn thing. Maybe when I get back out there and run your butt for ten miles, Private, you'll wake up!"

He slammed the phone back on the hook, then muttered several choice curse words at the instrument hanging on the kitchen wall.

"Something wrong, son?"

Nick jerked his head around to see his father standing directly behind him. No doubt the older man had heard at least part of the phone call he'd just made.

"I, uh—was trying to talk to my commanding officer. But apparently he's not there," Nick said a little sheepishly.

"Is there some important reason you need to talk to him this minute?"

Knowing S.T. had never liked to see his son's hot temper out of control, Nick drew in a steadying breath and tried to calm himself. "I wanted to see if I could get my leave extended a few more days."

S.T. suddenly laughed. "That's hard to figure. Why do you want to stay around here when you're so miserable?"

Was his mood that obvious? Nick wondered. He'd been trying so hard to act as if everything was hunky-dory. Apparently he wasn't any better at acting than he was at keeping his cool with inept privates.

"Dad, I'm not miserable, I'm…"

He didn't know how to go on. Fortunately, his

father didn't ask him to. Instead, the older man put his arm around Nick's shoulder and gave it an affectionate shake.

"Come on, son. I think you need to get out of here for a while."

Nick nodded and followed his father outside, where they climbed into S.T.'s pickup. The older man didn't say anything while he started the engine, then headed the truck down a track that led to what the family referred to as the east field. Nick was surprised at his father's silence. In the past, S.T. would have already lowered the boom and demanded Nick give him a reason for his behavior. Now he seemed to realize Nick needed a few moments to cool off and collect himself.

"I'm sorry you had to hear all that on the phone," Nick said finally.

S.T.'s grin was a wry one. "Now why should you be sorry about that? You think your old man never gets angry?"

Nick shrugged, then let out a tense breath. "Not like I do."

This brought a low chuckle from S.T. "Don't ever ask your mother that question. She might tell you differently."

"You never did like me losing my temper," Nick reminded him.

S.T. arched a brow at his son. "I never did like some of Sam's bad habits either. But we're not here to talk about that. So tell me what's really bothering you. And don't give me something about a private that needs waking up. You deal with that sort of problem every day."

Nick stared out the window at the flat river-bottom land. The remnants of a hegari crop had been turned into the roughly tilled soil. Nick knew that when the weather grew warmer and planting season approached, Sam would have this whole field disked to the texture of dark, rich powder. It would take days of work, but Sam had the patience and determination to do it—two things that Nick desperately needed now.

"No. It isn't about that. It's—" How could he talk to his father about Allison? The army had taught him to discipline his emotions, especially when, as a soldier, he found himself in a difficult situation. It was a means of survival. But right now, Nick wasn't so sure he could survive without Allison in his life.

"It's about Allison, isn't it? You want to marry her."

Nick jerked his head around. "Who told you that? Mother?"

"No. Kathleen did. But she really didn't need to. I'd already guessed."

"Kathleen! Hell, I suppose everybody in this family knows more about me than I do!"

"Just hold on, son. There's no need to get all defensive. We're just worried about you, that's all."

Nick passed a hand over his face. "Well, you needn't be."

S.T. gently braked the truck, which slowly rolled to a stop in the middle of the field. After killing the motor, he looked over at his son. "You're a part of this family, Nicholas. What affects you affects all of us."

Nick's features went rigid and unmoving. "I'm sorry I can't handle my love life the way Sam has. I guess he's got me there, too."

S.T. frowned, then snorted. "Oh hell, this isn't about what Sam can or cannot do. I don't know why you always want to bring Sam in on your problems."

Nick shook his head. "Maybe because he always seems to be in them no matter what I do!"

"Nick, you're—"

"Do you know what Allison said to me? She said I only wanted to marry her because Sam had gotten married, and I want to be like Sam."

S.T. thoughtfully studied his son. "Is that true?" he asked gently.

The compassion in his father's voice made the anger suddenly drain out of Nick.

"No. It isn't true. I really love her, Dad. I know that we met only a few days ago, and maybe that seems crazy. And maybe it's not the way my sensible brother would have done things. But that doesn't mean my feelings for Allison are any less strong than what Sam feels for Olivia."

"I didn't think they were," S.T. told him. "And as far as Sam handling his love life, if you'd been here during the Thanksgiving holiday, you would have seen your brother agonizing over Olivia. Hellfire, it took him four years to finally get the woman he loved."

Nick looked at his father. "We both know I don't have the patience Sam has."

S.T. folded both arms across his barrel of a chest. "What does that mean?"

Shaking his head, Nick looked back out the window at the fields around them. "Oh, come on, Dad, I'm a grown man. I can face the truth."

S.T. frowned with confusion. "What truth?"

Nick couldn't look at him. In fact, he wished he hadn't let his tongue run away with him. But now that he'd started this he might as well see it to the end, he thought. "That I was always second best to Sam. Hell, I guess even Allison can see it. She thinks Sam is great husband material. But good ol' Nick isn't even in the running."

"Is that what you really think?"

Nick turned to meet his father's gaze head-on. "It's true, isn't it? Just look around us. Sam runs the Gallagher farm now, not me."

S.T. spouted a string of curse words before he said, "You didn't want to be a farmer."

Nick ran a weary hand around the back of his neck. "No. But I wanted to believe I could have been one anyway."

A light suddenly dawned in S.T.'s eyes. "Nick, I don't know what you've thought all these years. But I've never saw you as second best."

Nick's eyes were full of doubt. "Sam was—"

"Sam was always good at farming. That's what he was meant to be. But when you went into the army, it finally made me see that I was wrong to try to turn you into a farmer or a lawyer or something that wasn't right for you."

"You always called me a rebel."

S.T. grinned. "You are, aren't you? But that doesn't mean you're bad. Or that you're any less my son. And as for what you're doing now, well, I think you've made a hell of a soldier. What's more, I think you know it, too."

Nick's laugh was short and reluctant at first, but by the time his father reached over and boxed him gently on the arm, he was grinning, too.

"Yeah, I guess I am pretty good at what I do."

"Damn right. And as for Allison, well, son, I think you just need to back off a little. She's gun-shy and you tend to come on a might strong at times."

Nick's expression was full of love as he looked

back at his father. "I guess you've always known me, haven't you?"

As S.T. chuckled, a hint of moisture glazed his eyes. "I may not always have known you, son. But I've always loved you."

# Chapter 13

Grandmother Lee is right, Allison thought later that morning as she pulled into her driveway. She couldn't keep the ring Nick had given her. Not unless she had intentions of marrying him. And she didn't. She couldn't. Nick just wasn't the right man for her.

Inside the house, she removed Ben's coat and settled him at the kitchen table with a glass of fruit juice. But all the while she moved around the room, picking up dirty dishes and odds and ends, her heart was setting up a painful howl. She loved Nicholas Gallagher. So why couldn't she marry him?

Because he was rash and impulsive, she silently argued. Having a family would bore him. Why, the word *marriage* had probably never entered his head until he'd come home to be Sam's best man, she thought.

The silent arguing continued until Allison finally went to her bedroom and dug out the velvet ring box she'd hidden under a stack of undergarments.

It was not a traditional engagement ring, she thought, a wan smile curving her lips as she stared down at the emerald and diamonds. But then she'd learned rather quickly that Nick was an untraditional man.

The sound of the telephone broke into Allison's thoughts. Quickly she left the bedroom and went to answer it before Benjamin decided to pick up the receiver.

"Hello."

"Allison, it's me," Kathleen said in a rush.

Allison went stock-still. Nick's sister was the last person she expected to be on the line. "What is it? Is something wrong?"

"Yes! Nick is going to the airport to catch a plane back to Fort Sill. You've got to stop him."

"Stop him! But I—"

"I'll be over there in just a minute to watch Ben."

Before Allison could say another word, Kathleen had hung up the phone.

Nick was leaving? Dazed by the news, Allison slowly put the receiver back in place. Why was he going? Was he planning to just leave, without a word to her? Why not, Allison? she answered herself. As far as Nick is concerned it's over between the two of you. He offered you his love and you threw it back at him. He probably doesn't ever want to see you again.

The finality of that thought made her shudder with fear. She couldn't let that happen!

Allison had barely gotten her coat on and grabbed her purse when Kathleen burst through the front door.

"He went west on the county road, but I'm not sure after that," she said in a breathless rush.

"But why is he going? I thought he didn't have to leave until tomorrow evening."

Kathleen waved her hand in a dismissive way. "There's no time for that now. If you love him, go. Stop him." She propelled Allison out the front door. "And don't worry about Ben. I'll be right here with him until you get back."

*If she loved him.* The words raced through her head as she hurried to her car. Oh yes, she loved him! And that was all that truly mattered. She had to let him know before he went away.

Snow was still packed on the dirt road leading from the farm. Allison was forced to drive slowly or risk sliding into the ditch. But much to her relief, she found the major highway leading into Fort Smith had been cleared.

With dry asphalt in front of her, she stepped down on the gas pedal and steered the car into the fast lane.

With a little luck she might be able to overtake Nick before he turned onto the airport road.

Reaching for the dash, Nick switched on the radio. He might as well hear a little music. Maybe it would help put him in a better frame of mind before he caught the military transport plane that would take him back to Fort Sill.

He hated to go. But if things worked out as he planned, and his commanding officer would grant him another week's leave, he could be back here in Fort Smith by tomorrow.

His talk with his father had opened Nick's eyes in many ways, and even though he was hurting over Allison's rejection, he felt like a new man where his family was concerned. Before, he'd always felt like an outsider, a rebel who'd been shunned, only tolerated. But S.T. had made him see that that concept had been all twisted.

Nick smiled to himself as he thought about the big, burly man. His father was wise. Nick had never doubted that. And he had said that Allison needed more time.

Well, she probably wouldn't consider a week very much time, but to a soldier it was a long vacation. And Nick intended to use every minute of it to convince Allison that he was serious about marriage. If she thought he'd given up on her, she was going to be in for a surprise.

The blare of a horn drew his attention and he automatically glanced into his rearview mirror. Stunned, he looked again. Was that Allison behind him?

Was he going to stop? Allison wondered as she gripped the steering wheel and peered at the red sports car in front of her. Was he so angry with her that he wouldn't look back, or give her another chance?

When his turn signal suddenly started to blink and the car began to slow down, Allison didn't know whether she was shaking with relief or with anticipation. Either way, it was an effort just to steer the car onto the side of the highway.

She was still fumbling with her seat belt when Nick jerked the car door open.

"Allison! What are you doing?"

With a little sob, she pushed aside the tangled belt and climbed out beside him. "Oh, Nick, I thought I was going to miss you—and then I thought you wouldn't stop because you…"

She was visibly trembling and her face was white. Unable to imagine what had put her in such a state, Nick quickly took her by the arm and led her around to the front of the car, where they would be farther away from the dangerous whiz of traffic.

"Allison, is something wrong?" he asked quickly.

She shook her head, then changed her mind and began to nod it up and down. "I—Kathleen said you were leaving. I couldn't let you go without telling you—"

His hands gripped her shoulders. "Telling me what?" he asked desperately.

"That…" Her eyes were on his face, drinking in the lean, strong features, the blue eyes that had sparkled at her that very first night they'd met. How had she ever thought she could let this man walk out of her life? In these few short days he had become her life. She knew that now.

"That I do want to marry you, Nick," she burst out. "I want it more than anything!"

The grave look on his face was swiftly replaced with wondrous joy. "You really mean it? You want to marry me?"

Happiness was flooding through her as she nodded back at him. "Yes. I want to marry you."

"When? Soon?"

His eagerness was infectious. With a breathless laugh, she reached out and locked her fingers around his biceps. "As soon as possible," she promised.

With a yelp of happy laughter he lifted her off her feet. "Thank God for my meddling, matchmaking sister!" he exclaimed as he hugged Allison close against his heart.

"What—"

Nick silenced her question with a kiss, which Allison found was just as addictive as his joy and excitement. When he lifted his lips, she pulled him back down and kissed him again.

"Come on, let's get out of the wind and out of view," he murmured after several passing cars honked at them.

Once they were inside Nick's car, Allison put her hand against his chest before he had a chance to draw her into his arms.

"Now what is this about your sister? She said you were leaving for Fort Sill. Isn't that true?"

Grinning, Nick nodded. "Yes. It is true. But apparently she didn't tell you that I was planning on coming back tomorrow."

Totally bewildered, Allison stared at him. "You were coming back? Tomorrow? But—"

"Oh, Allison, did you honestly think I could just walk away from you without a word?"

"I thought…" She paused as he took her hand between his. "When I told you I couldn't marry you, I was telling myself it was over between us. That I'd never see you again. Then Grandmother reminded me that I had to give the ring back to you, and the more I thought about it and you, and—oh, Nick," she said with a groan, "when Kathleen said you'd gone it shocked the blinders from my eyes. I was so afraid of making the same mistake I'd made in the past that I almost made an even bigger one—letting you go from my life. I'm just thankful your sister could see the truth."

He pulled her into his arms and pressed his face into her windswept hair. "So am I. Otherwise I might have spent weeks or months trying to convince you that my love for you is real." He pulled back to look at her. "Allison, I hope you believe me now when I tell you I want to be your husband. I want to be Benjamin's father, and the father of our own children."

She took his face between her hands, and as she looked into his eyes, she knew that she would never doubt this man or his love. He might have come into her life like a whirlwind, but she knew he was here to stay. "You don't have to convince me anymore, Nick. All you have to do is love me."

"My pleasure, darling," he whispered, drawing her lips to his.

"So, do you still have to leave? Today?"

He nodded and the disappointment on her face thrilled him. "I want to go back and talk to my commander about getting another week off, maybe two. Mother always throws a New Year's Eve party, and Sam and Olivia will be home from Colorado by then. We can make it into our engagement party. What do you say?"

Earlier, when Kathleen called, Allison had unwittingly dropped the ring box into her sweater pocket. Now she drew it out and handed it to Nick. "I say I love you," she told him, the smile on her face full of sweet promises. "And I'll be waiting here for you whenever you do get back."

He put the ring on her left hand, then pressed her palm against his lips. "The new year is coming. And so is our life together," he whispered, his eyes shining with love.

She circled her arms around his neck and pressed her cheek against the beat of his heart. "Yes," she murmured happily. "A new year, a new life. Starting now, and lasting forever."

\* \* \* \* \*

# REQUEST YOUR
# FREE BOOKS!

## 2 FREE NOVELS
## FROM THE ROMANCE COLLECTION
## PLUS 2 FREE GIFTS!

**YES!** Please send me 2 FREE novels from the Romance Collection and my 2 FREE gifts (gifts are worth about $10). After receiving them, if I don't wish to receive any more books, I can return the shipping statement marked "cancel." If I don't cancel, I will receive 4 brand-new novels every month and be billed just $5.99 per book in the U.S. or $6.49 per book in Canada. That's a saving of at least 25% off the cover price. It's quite a bargain! Shipping and handling is just 50¢ per book in the U.S. and 75¢ per book in Canada.* I understand that accepting the 2 free books and gifts places me under no obligation to buy anything. I can always return a shipment and cancel at any time. Even if I never buy another book, the two free books and gifts are mine to keep forever.

194/394 MDN FELQ

Name                          (PLEASE PRINT)

Address                                                          Apt. #

City                          State/Prov.                       Zip/Postal Code

Signature (if under 18, a parent or guardian must sign)

Mail to the **Reader Service:**
**IN U.S.A.:** P.O. Box 1867, Buffalo, NY 14240-1867
**IN CANADA:** P.O. Box 609, Fort Erie, Ontario L2A 5X3

Not valid for current subscribers to the Romance Collection
or the Romance/Suspense Collection.

**Want to try two free books from another line?**
**Call 1-800-873-8635 or visit www.ReaderService.com.**

* Terms and prices subject to change without notice. Prices do not include applicable taxes. Sales tax applicable in N.Y. Canadian residents will be charged applicable taxes. Offer not valid in Quebec. This offer is limited to one order per household. All orders subject to credit approval. Credit or debit balances in a customer's account(s) may be offset by any other outstanding balance owed by or to the customer. Please allow 4 to 6 weeks for delivery. Offer available while quantities last.

**Your Privacy**—The Reader Service is committed to protecting your privacy. Our Privacy Policy is available online at www.ReaderService.com or upon request from the Reader Service.

We make a portion of our mailing list available to reputable third parties that offer products we believe may interest you. If you prefer that we not exchange your name with third parties, or if you wish to clarify or modify your communication preferences, please visit us at www.ReaderService.com/consumerschoice or write to us at Reader Service Preference Service, P.O. Box 9062, Buffalo, NY 14269. Include your complete name and address.

# FAMOUS FAMILIES

**YES!** Please send me the *Famous Families* collection featuring the Fortunes, the Bravos, the McCabes and the Cavanaughs. This collection will begin with 3 FREE BOOKS and 2 FREE GIFTS in my very first shipment— and more valuable free gifts will follow! My books will arrive in 8 monthly shipments until I have the entire 51-book *Famous Families* collection. I will receive 2-3 free books in each shipment and I will pay just $4.49 U.S./$5.39 CDN for each of the other 4 books in each shipment, plus $2.99 for shipping and handling.* If I decide to keep the entire collection, I'll only have paid for 32 books because 19 books are free. I understand that accepting the 3 free books and gifts places me under no obligation to buy anything. I can always return a shipment and cancel at any time. My free books and gifts are mine to keep no matter what I decide.

268 HCN 0387    468 HCN 0387

Name _____ (PLEASE PRINT) _____

Address _____ Apt. # _____

City _____ State/Prov. _____ Zip/Postal Code _____

Signature (if under 18, a parent or guardian must sign)

## Mail to the **Reader Service:**
**IN U.S.A.:** P.O. Box 1867, Buffalo, NY 14240-1867
**IN CANADA:** P.O. Box 609, Fort Erie, Ontario L2A 5X3

FFBPA12

# *Reader Service*.com

## Manage your account online!

- Review your order history
- Manage your payments
- Update your address

---

*We've designed
the Reader Service website
just for you.*

---

## Enjoy all the features!

- Reader excerpts from any series
- Respond to mailings and
  special monthly offers
- Discover new series available to you
- Browse the Bonus Bucks catalogue
- Share your feedback

*Visit us at:*

# ReaderService.com